Here is a saucy tale of romance and secrets set against the elegance of 19th century Paris and London—the tale of an innocent abroad caught in the midst of intrigue, diplomacy, and danger. . . .

Also by Sarah Carlisle:

WIDOW AUBREY

CLEOPATRA'S CARPET

MLLE. CECIE

Sarah Carlisle

FAWCETT COVENTRY • NEW YORK

MLLE. CECIE

Published by Fawcett Coventry Books, a unit of CBS
Publications, the Consumer Publishing Division of CBS Inc.

ISBN: 0-449-50038-1

Printed in the United States of America

First Fawcett Coventry printing: April 1980

10   9   8   7   6   5   4   3   2   1

One

The sword flashed out in a dazzling display of fencing technique. "Take that, you French villain, and that!" The blade sank into the red velvet, slashing it to ribbons with a satisfying rip that could be heard clear across the room. "You see how I have parried that last thrust rather deftly, Cousin? I have been masterly, masterly! That poor Frog never stood a chance."

The only other person in the room, a young lady of nearly eighteen, stood cowering behind the velvet upholstered chair, giggling. "There was nothing for you to parry, as well you know, Peter."

Mr. Peter Pendyne grinned down at his second cousin, or was she his third?, and said, "That's not fair, Cecie. I have done a magnificent job, only you are incapable of appreciating it."

"Still, the chair has offered little resistance. You ought to be showing me your prowess with a real Frenchman, not the upholstery."

"As you are very well aware, your mama would not permit such a person to set foot in her parlor. For that matter, the whole countryside would object most strenuously if any Frenchie were to so much as enter the district. I must make do with what I have!"

Cecie looked as if she were going to protest such a cowardly excuse, but, peeking around the side of the chair back, her eyes beheld the full splendor of Peter's attack.

"Oh, no, Peter! The upholstery! You have quite slashed it to pieces. Mama will be so distraught! You have no idea how difficult it is to get good French silk velvet anymore, now that we are at war with France again." It was June of 1805, the beginning of a perfect summer day, a precious English rarity. Great Britain had proclaimed war against France some two years before, but it was still an exciting topic of conversation and speculation, especially in coastal areas exposed to the threat of invasion. Little had actually happened; although now that the man Bonaparte had crowned himself the winter before, making it an Imperial invasion, the excitement had risen to a fever pitch.

Peter was more concerned with Lady Penrith's reaction to the damage. She was Cecie's mother and the chatelaine of Penrith Hall, and a woman not to be crossed. He eyed the torn velvet, knowing full well that the term distraught would barely begin to describe that good lady's reaction to the violation of her prized wing-backed armchair. There was little chance of a reprieve from her anger. "The stuff was rather old anyway, wasn't it?"

"Yes, it was a trifle shabby. Mama meant to buy more velvet to replace it years ago, but this war took her by surprise."

Peter grinned at the thought of anything interfering with Lady Penrith's plans. He guessed that nothing short of war would have been sufficient to do so. "Perhaps I could replace it?" he offered.

His companion shook her head. "That is precisely the point! Only French silk will do, you know, and it is impossible to come by in these times."

"There must be some about, surely! A London draper would have it." His optimism was ignored by the girl.

"You might be so fortunate to find some, but it will cost dearly. And I doubt that there is any to be had. Mama has been writing off to all the best clothiers and drapers and every reply she has ever received has been most discouraging. She had resigned herself to making do with what she already had, shabby or not!" Cecie sat down on the window seat nearest the mutilated chair and looked at it with apprehension clear on her face. Not even the fact that it was a perfect day, warm and sunny, the first since spring had arrived in Cornwall, comforted her. The sunshine playing on the muslin ruffles of her sleeves went unnoticed while she examined the chair, dismayed with just how little of the velvet was left.

"Could it be mended?"

She sighed, not bothering to answer such a foolish question.

Peter shrugged his shoulders. "Well, I shall just have to face her and confess to what I have done. As you well know, it won't be the first time I have been in her bad graces! I have always managed to change her mind before."

The fact that her cousin had some five and twenty years of experience with getting into and out of trouble at Penrith Hall failed to comfort her.

"She will say that I encouraged your exuberance in this, I know she will!"

"What difference does that make? It never bothered her before, that you were audience to my misdeeds, for she always knew where to place the blame."

"It makes all the difference in the world! I am a young lady now. Mama has been discussing this most carefully with me. I have promised her that I will begin to behave with more decorum, now that I am so near my first Season."

"That should take a lot of practice, getting you ready for a London debut," he teased.

She failed to be amused. "It is just that I have given her my most particular assurances that I would be quiet and ladylike. She will say that I have conducted myself like a hoyden."

"Now, now. . . ."

"You would not have behaved so in the presence of a young lady of quality, as well you know." She was now close to tears.

"Cecie, you *are* a young lady of quality. No one can deny that. The Pendynes have been lords hereabouts since Tudor times and we are all frightfully respectable. It's just that because you are my cousin, I treat with you in a way that is informal. . . ."

"You mean familiar!"

"You are the most stubborn girl I know! Your mother can't expect to turn you into a society lady overnight. That would be asking too much!"

His words, meant to comfort, only stung the girl to a sharp retort. "I am every bit a lady, now that I am nearly eighteen! I will not have you treat me as a child any longer, Peter."

Peter appreciated that he had made a mistake in tactics, but on the whole he preferred to deal with a spitfire rather than a watering can. "You were prancing about and giggling just as you have always done, and you well know it!" he charged her.

Cecie refused to admit the truth of this statement and rose to her feet to defend herself, her cheeks a becoming rose, her eyes sparkling. Her physical resemblance to her cousin was remarkable at that moment: she shared with him the family coloring and the temper that went with the bright, curly auburn hair. But in her indignation she was unaware of anything more than the teasing he continued to inflict on her, just as he had done all through her childhood.

It was at this moment that Lady Penrith, attracted by the sound of angry voices, entered the room, intent on restoring the young people to peace.

"Whatever is this all about? You can't be squabbling again, you have only been together an hour, if not less! Such conduct is most unbecoming, Cecie," she told her daughter with firmness. In the last part of her scolding she was less than truthful, for Cecie had rarely looked as well as she did standing in the morning sunlight, blue eyes sparkling. Lady Penrith nearly caught her breath as she glimpsed the girl's full beauty, proud that such a lovely young lady was her own child, but determined not to turn the girl's head.

Faced with her mother, Cecie's thoughts turned to the far more serious matter at hand. "We have just been playing, Mama."

"You are a bit old for the rough and tumble of such games, darling," her mother said with more sympathy than the two young people had expected. "You must remember that, Cecie. It is all very well to treat Peter as if he were your brother, he has been your friend all your life, but you must not allow yourself to be drawn into unbecoming behavior. I can no longer blame Peter solely for your escapades. You are old enough to begin regulating your own conduct."

"It is really all my fault, Lady Penrith," Peter hastened to assure the matron. "I was just showing Cecie some of the swordplay I had learned from a brother officer."

10

"Swordplay? In my home? Peter, how could you!"

"But this room was once used as a fencing hall, ma'am. Those old plans you showed me but last week mark it as such quite clearly." He smiled at her, taking her hand in his own and exerting all of his considerable charm.

Lady Penrith, torn between her pride in the history of her husband's fine home and her sense of decorum, began to weaken. Then a chance glance of proprietorship around the room revealed the horror of her prize armchair, sitting desolate near the fireplace.

"My chair! The upholstery! All that lovely silk torn to shreds! What have you done to it? I shall never get more cloth like that, never, not while that monster Bonaparte roams through Europe." She moved to hover over the victim in an agitated fashion, twitching at the ribbons on the seat.

"I shall replace it, I swear to you, Lady Penrith! You have my word of honor, as a gentleman."

His promise failed to impress her. "Peter, you silly ninny, it is irreplaceable! How could you have done such a thing? And you, Cecie, why didn't you stop him? Such desecration! Such wanton destruction! It isn't enough that you have drawn your sword in my parlor, an act that no gentleman would ever dream of, even in jest! No, you have also wreaked havoc on my most valuable piece of furniture! Why, I brought that chair with me when I first married Penrith,

11

and it had been in my grandmother's drawing room when she was first married."

"The chair itself is still quite sound, Mama," Cecie said.

"But without a decent covering it is unusable, as well you know!" Her daughter cringed under the full weight of the lady's just anger and Peter hastened to draw the fire back to himself.

"I daresay that there are other ways of getting the material replaced, Lady Penrith."

"Whatever can you mean? Every draper and mercer in London has sold out his stock of quality French silk long ago, and anything less than that will not do. You may not be aware of it, young man, but the factories at Lyons produce the most beautiful silk in the whole world. I will not have less in my home!"

"We could put a needle-point cover on it, Mama," her daughter suggested, "I will do the stitching."

Such a sacrifice failed to soften Lady Penrith. "You know very well that if we rely on you to stitch sufficient canvas to cover the chair, the French monster will have solved the whole problem for us by dying of old age. No, really, Cecie!"

Peter spoke in a voice rather louder than usual, hoping to gain some control over the situation. "What I meant to say, Lady Penrith, is that there are ways of getting the material from France that don't include London merchants."

This only incensed the lady further. "You cannot mean those smugglers, Peter! I will not permit you to deal with such a ruffian lot as they, people who are violating the laws of the kingdom in such a treasonous way. If you purchase anything from them, you will be subverting the war plans of the government!" she scolded grandly. "I will not permit it! Those outlaws are taking gold out of England into France and carrying vital secret information to the enemy. It is not to be tolerated." For a moment she truly looked as if she were capable of stopping the man towering before her, and any number of smugglers, with her own puny stature, such was the hauteur she commanded when she drew herself to her full five feet of height.

"There are likely to be all sorts of people hoarding valuable stuff. Why, Aunt Emmet has trunks full of things she has bought with no intention of using, and I am sure that she is but one of many such people." He smiled with his usual easy friendliness, successfully hiding his guile from the lady. Only Cecie, who knew him better than anyone, was suspicious.

"Your Aunt Emmet?" Lady Penrith appeared to be much struck with this reminder of that elderly lady's habits. "I had never given her a thought. And now that I put my mind to it, there are probably some trunks in the attic full of all sorts of bolts of cloth. With Cecie coming out next spring, we will need every scrap of fashionable material to provide her with a decent wardrobe. Why that monster had to choose *this* spring to make war, and not that two years hence, I will never understand."

Peter, seeing that he had her thoughts on a safe path for the moment, nodded his vigorous agreement as she continued to rail against her favorite enemy. The fact that it had been the British government that had declared war was not mentioned during the next few minutes. One did not question one's government. He soon had his relative soothed into an agreeable frame of mind, and then seized the first opportunity to carry off young Cecie for a gallop over the south pasture. They left Lady Penrith directing her anger against the French across the Channel.

Two

Cecie mulled over her cousin's promise while she handled her spirited mount over a low stone wall. She was suspicious of the explanation he had given her mother, thinking his words over glib with self assurance. Lady Penrith, for all her affection toward the young man, would never have noticed the slight quirk around his eyes that her daughter had seen and interpreted with suspicion. In this, Cecie had the advantage of an almost sibling relationship with Peter and she always knew when he was up to no good.

Peter was the only son of her father's cousin and nearest male relation, Mr. Robert Pendyne of Pendyne Manor. As Cecie had no brothers, nor any sisters for that matter, it had long been taken for granted that the title and the estates would one day go to Peter, less a generous dowry for the girl, and the young man, although blessed with an affectionate mother and father of his own, had been encouraged to spend as much time as he wished at Penrith Hall. Lord Penrith had lavished attention on him and such advantages as he was well able to afford, being rather more comfortably placed in the world than Mr. Robert Pendyne, a gentleman of sufficient means for the luxuries of life, but with three very young daughters to provide for one day. Penrith's affection was equally distributed between Lady Cecilia, his daughter, and young Peter, and the children had been permitted to play as much together as the difference in their ages would permit.

Peter was some seven years older than Cecie, but he had always treated her kindly, teasing her affectionately and allowing her to tag along behind him with commendable patience whenever he was on a jaunt suitable for one so young and of the weaker sex. His own sisters were even younger than she and rarely entered into his thoughts except when actually underfoot.

Theirs had been a happy companionship through the woods and streams between their homes, when Peter's visits from school and later the army permitted it. In many ways he was her hero, the person who had taught her to ride a horse and even shoot a pistol, but he was also a tease and a practical joker. Their affection for one another had deepened over the last few months as they spent more time together while he was home on furlough.

They had reached a headland overlooking a particularly magnificent stretch of rocky coastline, and he called to her to dismount. A packet retrieved from his coat pocket revealed his foresight: he had brought a snack of apples and cheese to refresh them as they rested and enjoyed the view. Cecie had consumed most of the apples before she was sure enough of her own thoughts to attempt putting them into words.

"Do you really think that your Aunt Emmet will have material suitable for re-upholstering the chairs, Peter?" She threw out the question, pretending an elaborate indifference to all but the spray being tossed up against the rocks below them by the pounding surf. Her pose failed to deceive him.

His answer was wary. "I am not sure, Cecie, but I will try there first."

"And if she does not have it? What will you do then?"

He laughed at her and then tossed one of her apple cores into a pool of roiling sea far below. "Why do you worry so about it? The day is magnificent, you should be enjoying it. Isn't the smell of flowers and sea air exhilarating?"

"It would appear that you find it so," she commented sourly, referring to his too high spirits.

"Look over there. Doesn't that cloud look like a camel? Can you see how its back is hunched and its long legs stick out so? And there is even a tail."

She glanced in the direction he pointed and answered with a shrug. "It looks more like a storm cloud to me."

"All the more reason to enjoy the day while it

lasts," he answered, his expression still gay. "You never have any spirit of romance, Cecie, a sad lacking in a young lady. Why do I always have to come up with the farfetched ideas and wild imaginings? You can't even produce a good story about whom you will marry."

Cecie, who strongly suspected that her mother would consider such talk on her part ill bred, was uninterested. "That is a long way off, and you know it well, Cuz. I have not even been presented yet."

"Come, even May, my youngest sister, was boring me with her prattling just last night. She is going to marry a prince and be a great lady, and have her own coach and horses and as many cream puffs after dinner as she wants, every night. Can't you match that?"

Irritated with his efforts to distract her from the important matter at hand, she tossed a chunk of cheese at him, shying it off his forehead. "You aren't paying me any attention anyway, Peter. Why should I spin fine tales for you? It would only be a waste of time, and you say you were bored with May's, in any case."

"What? A waste of time?" He sat up with mock indignation written on his face, brushing off the crumbs of cheese from his shoulder. "And what have I done to deserve a cheese tossed at my head? You should be thanking me for providing you with so much food. You ate nearly all of it."

She failed to rise to the bait. "That doesn't matter and it never has. You have always let me eat as much as I want and there was plenty left for you. Now, don't you dare to change the subject again, Peter. I have a very serious thing to discuss with you."

He sighed and returned his head to a soft tuft of grass. "What important things, love? I thought that the camel was rather important, myself. And don't all young girls long to talk about marriage? But as you aren't interested in either of those things, we'll talk about whatever you want."

"You must not go to the smugglers, Peter. I know that that is what you intend to do, no matter what you say. You can't fool me the way you did Mama."

"How severe you sound, Moppet."

She frowned into his smiling face and pressed on. "Peter, Mama is right, it would be highly improper for you to seek out the Gentlemen. Their trade is most dangerous to the safety of the country."

"Really? How do you know that?" he asked with courteous interest.

"I heard Papa talking with his friend Lord Carstairs, and they said that it was so. They should know, surely, for both sit in the House of Lords. They are part of the government, I am sure."

Peter, who knew that Lord Penrith had graced that august body with his presence only once, on the occasion of his presentation and maiden speech, which he treated as a social event of some importance, grinned even more wickedly.

19

"Well, anyway, Lord Carstairs attends. It would be wrong of you to consort with such ruffians. Their activities enable the French to send agents into England quite freely, so that they can spy on our coastal defenses and steal secrets and create all sorts of mischief, even kill people! Everyone knows that!"

Peter looked at her with an expression that was suddenly somber. "Perhaps you are right, Cecie. But I have given your mother my word, after all, and I think I know of a goodly crew of Gentlemen who are loyal to the King but in sad need of a little extra cash with which to pay his taxes. They won't include any spy smugglers, I assure you. Their cargo consists wholly of casks of brandy and wine and trunks of expensive luxuries, all of which give them more than enough profit to keep them from the temptation of more dangerous enterprises."

Cecie heard this with dismay, knowing that she had failed. She had never heard him utter such irresponsible nonsense before, and something about the corners of his eyes warned her that he might be teasing her in some way.

"Untaxed luxuries!"

Peter only shrugged.

She tried another tack. "That is all well and good, but Mama would be most distressed if you were to do so on her account. It is dishonorable of you to even consider it, Peter."

"More dishonorable than breaking my word to your mother?"

Now he *was* teasing her. "Much more dishonorable. Whatever has come over you, Cuz? How can it be that I, your little cousin, must teach you the right and wrong of it? In the past you were wont to set me on the straight path. Now our roles have changed."

"It's that regrettable lack of imagination on your part, Cecie, that makes it so. You have always seen things in such stark terms of right and wrong. Once I told you that this was such and such and that the other, you never forgot, and you are incapable of thinking of another way about it. In times of war, things change. . . ."

"Peter, I am ashamed of you! There is nothing good about smuggling, nothing at all! It violates the law and puts the whole country in terrible jeopardy. You, as an officer in the army, should appreciate all of this."

"Sometimes such things are a two-edged sword, Cuz," he said as he tossed the rest of the apple cores over the rocks. "Come along, Cecie. We must be riding back or you will be late for dinner, and that would never do. That terribly dull Dean Whittaker will be at table, or so your father warned me. I must get you back and then be off myself, before I am trapped into joining you."

"You still haven't answered me satisfactorily, Peter," Cecie grumbled, rising and brushing the grass from her blue serge riding habit.

Peter only seemed to notice her efforts to make herself tidy. "That shade of blue just matches your eyes, Cecie. You should wear it as often as you can. Tell your mother that I think so."

"She is already aware of that, I can assure you. Many of my dresses have this color about them!" Tears were sparkling in those same blue eyes and she forced him to look at her, demanding the answer to her question, without speaking a word.

Peter did look down at her face for a long moment, seeing the new maturity and being touched by her concern for his well being. With a sigh, he gave her a promise that he hoped would satisfy her. "Very well, Cuz. I promise that I will do nothing frivolous or for reasons of personal adventure or gain. You will always be proud of my motives, Cecie, of that I assure you."

She still looked doubtful as he ended this declaration. It was not quite what she had expected. There was that familiar warning inside her that he hadn't told her all of his thoughts, that something was being held back, whether to tease her or otherwise she could not tell at present.

"Will you swear at the Holy Well?" she asked him.

He was surprised by the vehemence of this unexpected request, but after a moment of thought, nodded his head in the affirmative. Without another word Cecie lead him along a faintly-marked path to an outcrop of rocks that looked impenetrable. A passage could be seen through the massive stone if one knew the proper angle of approach, and it was through here that Cecie passed. Once inside, they came to a spring bubbling up in the floor of the cavern. It was one of the many holy spots in Cornwall dedicated to some long forgotten Breton missionary sainted for his work among the heathens of the region centuries before. There, they knelt on the hard floor, and Peter repeated his oath to her, using much the same formula as he had earlier. After a long look at the water, Cecie nodded her satisfaction. It was a haven of their childhood, and therefore doubly sacred to her.

Once they were back in the bright sunlight, Peter's mood changed. "Come, I shall race you back!"

He ran over to where their tethered mounts were munching the long stalks of grass and spring flowers, and gestured to her impatiently to gather her skirts about her. Then, with a strong arm, he threw her into the saddle, tossed the reins up, and leaped onto the back of his own mount. In seconds they were galloping over the grassy slopes, choosing their way in places by following the remains of the old crosses that had once marked the path along the headlands. The manes of their horses streamed out in the wind and Cecie's hair and skirts whipped about her in the buffeting air. The race was close, for although Peter was the better horseman, Cecie's mount was a spirited one and the girl an easier weight to carry. But as always, Peter, just one pace ahead of her, arrived first in the stableyard of the Hall in a flurry of flying earthen clods, and won the race. They were both laughing and

23

in a carefree mood when he swung her off the mare and to the ground, their disagreement of the cliff forgotten.

It wasn't until late in July that Cecie remembered the promise he had made her. There arrived at the Hall a parcel addressed to her mother and accompanied by a sealed letter directed to that lady's attention. When the wrappings of paper were removed, Lady Penrith was delighted to find several bolts of magnificent velvet, of the finest French silk, in just the same shade that her old upholstery had been. True, the pattern of the cloth was somewhat different from what she had been accustomed to use, but she declared that to be a vast improvement. The accompanying note was from Peter Pendyne, saying that although his Aunt Emmet had failed to produce the needed material, she had told him of an aged crony of hers, one who was wont to join her for shopping sprees whenever they happened to be in London together, and Mrs. Emmet was sure that this lady had purchased yards and yards of the finest silk velvet but four years before, in a color that should match Lady Pendyne's needs. His second inquiry had produced the enclosed results and he hoped that they were satisfactory. He apologized for being unable to present the bolts himself, duty demanding his attendance with his regiment, but if there was any difficulty, she should but let him know. He ended diffidently, asking if this would do to discharge his debt.

It did, indeed. Within a few short days the armchairs were back in their places of honor, gracing the fireside, each covered in the valuable red French silk. Cecie would often sit on the window seat in that parlor and stare at them, an unhappy look on her face, but her loyalty to Peter forbade her to doubt the story he had told her mother about his gift. She would have to accept a very unsatisfactory situation until she could see him again.

Three

It was several weeks before Cecie next saw her cousin Peter, who had heretofore had all the time in the world, but was now gone from home for days on end on business.

Lord Penrith's birthday fell early in August, during some of the hottest of the summer's days. Despite the sultry atmosphere, or perhaps because it was as well to seize any opportunity to ignore the temperature, the day was an occasion for elaborate festivities at Penrith Hall. The servants were allowed to leave off their labors to celebrate their master's birthday, excepting the kitchen and serving staff who had to wait for their holiday at a time when there were fewer demands for their services. The front lawn of the estate was filled with laborers and the lesser tenants of the property, eating their fill and drinking innumerable tankards of ale from the barrels his lordship so thoughtfully provided. The house itself was crowded with the neighboring gentry, including the Pendynes of Pendyne Manor and Major Hugh Armstrong, the orphaned son of Lord Penrith's dearest boyhood friend.

It was not until late in the evening that the gifts were presented to the host. After the guests from outside the family had departed, well content with a banquet of saddle of beef, mutton, pork, three kinds of fish in four kinds of sauces, stews, ragouts, side dishes of vegetables, and a dessert of a sugary confection served with fruit, the presents were brought out. The family gathered in the red salon, once more resplendent now that the new velvet had been put to good use on the armchairs. There was much exclaiming over the handsome new furnishings while they sipped their wine or lemonade. Lord Penrith examined the prettily wrapped gifts appreciatively.

"Now, where shall I start? With this tiny little present from Cecilia? You cannot love me very much if the size of your gift is a measure to judge by." He smiled at her fondly, tweaking her cheek, while the assembled family laughed.

Her temper had started to flare before she realized that he was teasing her, but when Cecie answered him with a saucy quip, her cheeks were rosy and her eyes sparkled. "You know very well that it is the quality rather than the quantity of the gift that marks it value, Papa. The same can be said of love," and she leaned forward impulsively to kiss him.

"That is the best gift of all, that kiss," he said

with a laugh. "It is all I really wanted from you, daughter, valuable for the qualities of love it brings. It may seem a small thing to some, but as you have taught us, that is not how one judges its value."

Peter had been watching his little cousin and thinking, not for the first time, that perhaps he should no longer consider her so. "There will be many a young man who will seek such a gift, Cecie. Your papa and mama will have to be careful for you, to see that no one steals you away!"

Mr. Robert Pendyne nodded his agreement. "Damned pretty girl, Penrith. You'll have a flock of young men chasing after her, mark my words. She'll be the belle of the Season." Several people laughed again, but Hugh merely looked at her more closely, his eyes narrowed thoughtfully.

Cecie began to blush even more, and hid her embarrassment by turning back to her father. "Well, do open it, Papa!"

Smiling, he began to untangle the ribbon holding the paper to the tiny box, a task of some complexity given the knots that had been tied. "You have protected your valuable gift too well, Cecie."

"Here, let me," and she tore the ribbons off with a few deft tugs.

The box that the paper had hidden was beautiful in itself. She had skillfully embroidered tiny flowers on cloth that had then been bound to the long rectangular top and sides of the cardboard, displaying the yellow primrose of the

29

Pendyne family coat of arms in a field of blue. Lord Penrith passed the box around, pointing out its perfections to an appreciative audience, and continuing to exclaim until his impatient daughter bade him open it.

Lying inside was a stickpin decorated with another primrose, worked in gold, displaying a fine yellow diamond in its center. The gem, although small, was of the finest quality and sparkled in the light of the candelabra. A gasp of pleasure murmured through the people present.

"Why, thank you, puss. It is the handsomest thing I have seen in many a year." He leaned over to hug her and plant a kiss on her cheek.

"Mama helped me to arrange for it, Papa, but the idea was all my own."

"Well, then I must thank your mama, also, for her assistance," and he rose to lean over his wife's chair, gracing her cheek with an equally affectionate kiss.

"Our presents will seem pale in comparison!" Mr. Pendyne laughed from his place beside his wife. Despite his protest, he brought forward his own gift, a fine ebony walking stick, with unaffected good will and the unwrapping continued.

After an hour, Lord Penrith was surrounded by a clutter of paper and gifts that included an antique book on fox hunting, from Major Armstrong, a pair of finely-embroidered slippers, from his cousin's wife, and a fine enameled snuffbox from Lady Penrith. There remained to be unwrapped only a large box from Peter; his was by far the largest of the gifts. Lord Penrith indulged in a moment of gently shaking it and trying to guess at its contents, while the conversation bantered around him.

"It is definitely an example of quantity, Peter. I fear that Cecie has taken the wind out of your sails if you expect to impress our host with the size of whatever it is." Hugh Armstrong said this with a hint of malice, running his hand through his immaculate fair hair and then carrying it to a position a foot out from his waist. He stared down at it there, examining his five manicured fingers with curiosity, as if surprised to find them hanging from the end of his arm.

Peter kept a solemn look on his face. If the truth were told, he and Hugh had never had a good understanding between themselves, despite an acquaintanceship that stretched over many years. They had been rivals in school and rivals for the affection of Lord Penrith for so long that such a friendship as their patron wished for was beyond hope. "I had also hoped that the quality would account for something, Hugh, but it is all too obvious that little can compete with such fine gifts as the rest have brought this day. I can only pray that Lord Penrith will accept it in the affectionate spirit in which it is given and judge it accordingly."

There was a twinkle in Penrith's eye as he opened the box, and Cecie shushed her cousin imperiously so that all attention would be focused on the last of the gifts. As the paper was torn away, a handsome walnut veneer case was seen to be emerging.

"By Jove, I think I have an idea of what it is, Penrith, you lucky devil," Mr. Pendyne exclaimed.

His smile broadening, Lord Penrith fumbled with the key in the lock of the box, and then raised the lid of the case to reveal a handsome pair of flintlock pistols. Nestled in green felt lining, the steel and walnut of the weapons flashed with the gold and silver inlay of the decoration. Cecie pressed forward to examine the designs more closely.

"Look, Papa! There are dolphins and anchors here on this end. How pretty they are!"

Penrith weighed one of the pistols in his hand, appreciating its balance. "That is the buttcap, as you ought to know, love. This is one of the finest pistols I have ever seen, Peter. Thank you for your generous gift."

"And what a pretty conceit it is to have a nautical device on it, we live so near the sea," Lady Penrith added.

Hugh leaned forward to examine the other gun. "About sixteen inches in length. And it looks to be of French manufacture, Peter, hard to come by in times of war. Where did you get them?" His cool tone and raised eyebrows implied a degree of doubt in the propriety of such a gift, for this was a patriotic household and Hugh an active officer in His Majesty's service. The question was almost a demand.

Peter smiled and stepped into the circle of

candlelight illuminating Lord Penrith's chair. "I was fortunate enough to pick them up in London when last there. The man who sold the pistols to me was a French émigré of sorts. I understood from listening to what he *didn't* say that he had been caught out in some scheme to defraud the Quarter Master's office and had had to flee the country to avoid prosecution on charges of bribery and corruption. He told me that the set was manufactured by Nicolas-Noël Boutet in Versailles only a few years ago. Boutet has one of the finest reputations as a gunsmith and craftsman in the whole of France." He reached over to point out the manufacturer's mark.

"And of course you are well aware of such a thing, having spent so much of your time on the Continent while finishing your, ah, education," Hugh interposed.

Everyone tried to ignore his comment. "I think they are vastly pretty, Papa," Cecie said quickly.

"You must allow me to try them out some day soon, Penrith," Mr. Pendyne interjected.

Somehow the conversation continued on these pleasanter lines as each of the men, and even the ladies, found something to admire in the beautiful workmanship of the pistols and their case. After her initial comment, Cecie hung back from the discussion, trying to hide the confusion on her face.

As they were preparing to leave the room to partake of a light supper, Peter caught her arm and pulled her aside. "Not moping because your present might not have been the best, are you,

33

Cecie?" he asked with a grin. "You shouldn't, you know. I thought your father was inordinately pleased with the pin. He has stuck it into his coat and is wearing it this minute."

"It isn't a question of one being better than the other," she shot back in anger. "Your gift is not the sort of thing I would give Papa. For one thing, I don't understand guns all that well, for all I am a tolerable shot."

"And for another?" He was no longer smiling at her.

"For another, it is yet one more piece of French manufacture that you have brought into this house. You seem to be a veritable merchant of French goods, Peter. Are you planning to set up shop?"

Peter looked at her sharply, but smiled after a moment. "Far from that, Cecie. After all, a gentleman doesn't enter into trade."

"Not legitimate trade, in any case. But there seems to be some sort of fascination among the men of the surrounding district for trade of another sort. And I have heard that those merchants do call themselves 'Gentlemen!' It is said to be a very profitable business for those who participate in it. Is this so?"

"I have heard it said so, Cuz. But you forget that I gave you a promise not so long ago."

"I have forgotten no such thing. It is my disappointment in seeing a growing list of evidence that you have broken it that is causing me to question you now. I cannot rejoice in my father being the recipient of smuggled goods, no matter what the affection with which they are presented. Tell me, have you sunk so low as to use your own boat?"

Peter let a sigh escape and turned her around so that he could look straight into her eyes. "You will never have cause to doubt my word, Cecie. You are far too important to me for that. In fact, you have grown prettier than any other young lady of my acquaintance. I wish you would forget about this smuggling nonsense and think of your coming Season. It is most important to you and you should be enjoying the preparations for it. I want to see you shine when you arrive in London, so that people will appreciate you the way that I do." His face was suddenly very close to hers, and she pulled back with a start.

"There are other things that are far more important to me. Such as the honor of my family and friends."

"Cecie, could you not trust me? You have never had cause to doubt my word in the past, why do you suddenly begin to do so now?"

She looked at him shrewdly. "Because better than anyone else, I know you and your thoughts. And I know that there is something that you are hiding from me. You may be able to fool the others, but you can't pull the wool over my eyes. There is something of which you are ashamed, something that you feel compelled to hide, isn't there, Peter?" Her voice had taken on a trembling note, and he saw to his dismay that her eyes were brimming with unshed tears.

"There are many reasons for secrets, Cecie,

and not all of them dishonorable. Won't you trust me, love?"

"Oh, Peter, I don't know what to think. If only I could believe you!" She turned and fled up the stairs to her room, leaving him to make what excuses he could to the rest of the party for her absence.

As he turned from the hall, he nearly encountered another of the house guests. Major Armstrong had secreted his tall, heavy figure in the deep shadow cast by the curve of the stairway, an excellent listening post for any conversation conducted in the hall. His thoughts were a remarkable reflection of Cecie's accusations, and with perfect cynicism he determined to discover all that he could about Peter Pendyne's involvement in smuggling.

Four

Cecie's exasperated feelings were further irritated on the following morning when she chanced into the sewing room, a pleasant, sunny chamber in the back of her home. Here, a seamstress called down from London, was hard at work under the demanding supervision of Lady Penrith, creating gowns for Cecie's coming Season.

During the summer the materials used had been mulled muslin, striped and plain cottons, and fine wools, some untouched by embroidery, others covered with floral and animal motifs varied with occasional swags and arabesques. Cecie had been pleased with her gowns, unimpressed with her mother's promise that the truly elegant ones would be created by the most fashionable modistes in London; to her mind, what was being made in her own home was quite grand enough for her. But on that morning the character of the sewing room had changed. The simple English-made materials had been rudely set aside.

In their place were bolts and bolts of the finest velvets, silks, and satins. Her mother and the seamstress were fingering a particularly fine white damask covered with a design of wheat sheaves, discussing its suitability for a ball gown. Lady Penrith looked up when she heard her daughter enter the room and waved for her to join them.

"Cecilia, dear, do come and see what Peter brought over yesterday. He said it was a surprise for you, something he discovered while looking for my red velvet upholstery material. And just look what it is!" She spread her arms wide to indicate the bounty that was literally overflowing the chairs and tables of the room.

Everywhere she looked Cecie saw beautiful, expensive cloth. There was a bolt of saffron yellow striped silk gauze on the floor near her left foot. It partially covered another bolt of white pina cloth embroidered with multicolored silk floss and silver sequins and metallic thread. Valenciennes lace spilled into a pile of lilac gray silk; rich pale green velvet vied for attention next to it. Resting on the window seat silver, tinsel and gold threads were displayed against the dark blue of silk, sparkling in the sunlight. Silks, velvets, taffetas, lawn, gauzes, damasks, laces, muslins. Flowers, laurel sprays, birds, butterflies, arabesques, swags, fruit, scollery, bands. Silver and gold and tinsel threads, silk embroidery, fox fur trim, beaded lace. White and cream

38

and champagne and green and cerise and rose and chartreuse and sky blue and saffron and lilac and . . .

She was appalled.

"Whatever is it all doing here!" she protested in a faint voice.

Lady Penrith mistook the girl's reaction and proceeded to congratulate her on her good fortune. "You will be the luckiest girl of the Season, Cecilia. No one, absolutely no one, will have gowns such as yours. Just look at it all!"

"But I couldn't use it!"

Her eye lingered on a particularly bright red silk and Lady Penrith laughed her agreement. "No, you are quite right, that piece would never do for a young girl in her first Season. Much too bright. But we shall save what we can't use now for your trousseau. You will need as many bright and pretty shades as you can find for that, for a married lady is expected to use a greater variety of colors in her gowns and costumes than a maiden. Now, Morgan and I had just decided that the lighter shades and of course the whites and creams and champagne colors would be just the thing. We can use the velvet only for the most elaborate ball gowns, of course, but the silks and satins will do nicely for daytime costumes, if we handle them tastefully. I declare, I am tempted to see to all this myself, rather than bother with a London dressmaker. Morgan and I are in perfect agreement and we have already produced some lovely gowns for you. Don't you think this velvet will do nicely for your own ball?" She had turned back to the bolt she had been examining when her daughter entered the room, expecting the girl to follow her and voice her approval.

Cecie could only stare at her mother's back with dismay. Since the unfortunate scene in the hallway the night before, she had been wrestling with her conscience on the question of what to do about Peter. She had very nearly convinced herself that her suspicions were unfounded. After all, was it so unlikely that French goods could be found in some parts of London? The City was the trading hub of the world and ships from all over the globe put in there. What could be more natural than a Frenchman selling some of his property to raise cash in a crisis? Peter's story could have been nothing but the truth. Or so she had reasoned.

Her trust in him crumbled in the face of all this splendor. Surely all of these bolts of material, with a quality and style that outshone the more provincial English textiles, must be French. Where could he have gotten them?

"Mama, where did he say he had found all of them?" she asked over Lady Penrith's shoulder.

"Why, here and there while he was searching for that velvet for my chairs. The dear boy realized that these would be the very thing for all the gowns and dresses you will be needing. Look! He even brought some sable for a muff! Wasn't that thoughtful of him? He must have combed the countryside looking for all of this."

What could she say in view of her mother's trust and enthusiasm? Lady Penrith clearly believed whatever Peter Pendyne had told her, that the fabric had been come by honestly, by chance, that as a good friend and relative, Peter had seized the opportunity of helping his cousin in a most practical way. Lady Penrith wanted to believe it.

"It is unusual to find a young man of Peter's interests and experience who notices these fripperies that are so dear to a lady's heart," Lady Penrith said softly as she stroked the ivory plush. "It was very kind and considerate of him to help us by purchasing them for you."

"They must have cost him dearly."

"Yes, I fear they did. But he won't hear of accepting a single pence for them. In the ordinary way, I wouldn't allow it, but he is a family connection, of course, quite like a brother to you, and perhaps he will be much more."

"I can't possibly accept any of this material, Mama," Cecie protested again.

"Of course you can. I envy you your good fortune!" her mother insisted.

How could she be so naive? Cecie, anxious to have no part in what she considered an illegal operation, sought to disengage herself from a gift about which she knew too much. "Why don't you make use of it, Mama? I am quite content with my muslin and wools. They are far more suitable for a young lady than these rich fabrics, and you would look handsome in any one of

41

these materials. Take this saffron taffeta, for example; it would make a lovely ball gown for you." She reached over to the bolt she had noticed and pulled it out for inspection.

"You are a dear girl to be so generous, Cecie, but I would never dream of depriving you of this windfall. You will be the envy of every other debutante this coming Season and I will be so proud of you. So will your papa! You will look beautiful in every single gown we make, just you see."

Cecie had no intention of accepting the gift, but she could not reveal Peter's treachery to her doting mama. Peter Pendyne had suddenly raised himself to the ranks of the angels in Lady Penrith's eyes and Cecie hadn't the heart to disillusion her. No, she would do something about this herself, something that would put an end to this smuggling and repair what damage had been done as best she could. Peter would have to be stopped.

On the other hand, Lady Penrith attributed her daughter's lack of enthusiasm to girlish modesty and shyness. She knew that once Cecie had worn the fabulous gowns that were being planned for her, she would quickly accept them, despite her Miss-ish hesitation of the moment. It only wanted a little experience in the ways of the world to convince Cecie that Peter's gift had been a truly generous one, an outstanding gesture of help and support. Her growing conviction that Cecie was to be the belle of the coming Season had long been nurtured in her bosom; now she had tangible hope of seeing her ambition for the girl come to pass. Seizing a pale yellow muslin, she sought to enlist her daughter's enthusiasm.

"Look what I plan to do, Cecie. We will make you walking dresses and morning gowns out of the simpler fabrics, but decorate them with material in the bright colors. I think that that will be quite tasteful and unobjectionable. This satin saffron, for instance, can be made into a spencer that will look charming with the paler muslin. You just see if I am not right." Chatting happily, she unfolded her fashion plans to her unwilling child.

More than an hour passed before Cecie was able to escape the sewing room. What peace of mind she had found in the trusting presence of her mother was shattered by an encounter with Major Armstrong. That gentleman was entering the hallway as she reached the bottom step, just returned from a morning of riding if his clothes were any clue to his activities. Cecie tried to walk by him with a smile and a nod, anxious to find privacy in which to consider her plans for action, but Hugh seized her arm and detained her, his supercilious smile informing her that she was to take no offense at this treatment.

"Have you seen your new wardrobe materials, Cecie? Bolts and bolts of the finest French fabric. I congratulate you on your good fortune!"

She muttered her thanks and tried to pull

away, but Hugh would not release her arm.

"Peter is the kindest of cousins imaginable, I am sure," the man whispered down to her.

"He is most generous."

"Most generous. First your father, and then you, although he nearly repented the latter."

"Oh?" Cecie wished that this had happened and that Major Armstrong had never seen the fabric.

"He was in the act of carrying his booty out of the house when your mother chanced into the hallway."

"She did not tell me so."

"Clever man that he is, he changed direction and said he was walking in, not out."

"How silly. I am sure you are mistaken, sir."

"Oh, no, not that. I had watched his antics for some time. First the careful smuggling operation up to the sewing room early in the day, then the retreat after we had supped."

Cecie, her own guilty thoughts betraying her, went to Peter's defense. "Surely smuggling is too strong a term to be used. Peter must have been planning some sort of surprise."

"So he told Lady Penrith. He said that this delightful surprise was for your benefit, of course. What a pity you had retired so early to your bed! You missed the excitement, whether you call it smuggling or no. Does the booty meet with your favor?"

His repeated use of the word booty warned her. This time Cecie kept her temper in check, responding to Hugh's taunts in a more considered manner. "The fabrics are lovely. If you will excuse me, I am not feeling well."

"What? Another headache? Perhaps we should summon a surgeon to bleed you!" Hugh suggested. His malicious grin was more than she could bear, for in truth she did not feel well, and without another word, she freed herself from his grasp, twisting and jerking her arm, and fled.

Five

After much thought, Cecie put her plans into action that afternoon. She began by summoning her young maid to attend her.

"Molly, there is something very important I want you to do for me," she announced once the two girls were in the privacy of Cecie's bedchamber.

Molly, a plump country girl who had known Cecie all her life and was devoted to her, curtsied and nodded her head in vigorous assent. She expected nothing more complicated than an errand to Pendyne Manor, or perhaps the charge of a shopping trip to the nearby village of Austen's Chapel for some minor trinket; it was such that she was accustomed to.

"Molly, you have been seeing much of Willie Hobbins of late, I collect?"

The girl blushed and nodded her head, too embarrassed to consider the unusual nature of the query, and what it had to do with her task. "We be walking out some, Lady Cecie." A sudden thought struck her and she hastened to add, "It's all proper and respectable, my lady, that I assure you."

Cecie smiled at her and offered reassurance. "I am sure that it is all perfectly unexceptional, Molly. You are a good girl and your mama keeps a careful eye on you, as she should. It is this friendship with Willie that will prove helpful to me."

Molly was thoroughly confused by now, but she curtsied again and mumbled, "Yes, my lady. If you say so, my lady."

"Willie works with my cousin, Mr. Peter Pendyne, on his boat, doesn't he?"

"Yes, my lady, that he does."

"Good. It is about this boat that I wish to learn more. I want you to ask Willie certain questions for me. It is most important, and I don't want my cousin to hear of it."

"Yes, Lady Cecie." Molly's voice had grown more doubtful as her young lady's talk had continued. Cecie, noticing this mood in her cohort, realized that she must say something to allay the girl's suspicion that there was something seriously amiss. A sudden inspiration came to her aid.

"You see, it will be Mr. Peter's birthday in a few months, and I wish to give him some very special gift. I know that his boat is a source of great amusement to him and I thought to find

48

something that would remind him of it. But I know so little about boats and such," here she paused to smile in a shamefaced way, soliciting the sympathy of one female for the helplessness of another, "that I was hoping that your Willie would give me some clue."

Molly enthusiastically entered into the intrigue. A special birthday gift for Mr. Peter opened exciting possibilities for the young girl, offering confirmation of something that she and her Willie had discussed together on many occasions. She partook of her mistress's plans heart and soul.

"I could bring Willie to you here, my lady," she offered.

Cecie considered this a moment, then frowned. "No, if anyone were to see us talking together, they would wonder what we are about. I don't want to arouse suspicion or comment, you know. But you see Willie anyway, so it will be quite natural for the two of you to be together. You must ask him the questions for me."

The maid was much struck by the wisdom of this reasoning and acquiesced with another bob of her head. "You just tell me what it is you needs to know, my lady, and I will get Willie to tell me," she promised.

Cecie flashed her a pleased smile and began. "I would like to know where Mr. Peter takes the boat. I had thought that some sort of memento of a port he had visited might be suitable, a chart or something of that nature."

Molly, full of trust, nodded her understanding. "Place where they put into port."

"And I should like to know what sort of things Mr. Peter carries on his yacht. Does he ever seem to carry cargo?"

Molly accepted this without a murmur.

"And when has he sailed? And when will he sail again? Can you ask him all of this?"

"I can do more than that," Molly said with a giggle. "I can get him to answer me, too."

"Good girl. Now, when do you think you will be able to see Willie again? Will it be some time soon?"

Molly blushed again. "He were to take me to the evening service at Chapel this very day, Lady Cecie. I can ask him when he walk me home."

"That is much better than I'd hoped for, Molly. You are a dear girl to help me so, and you won't go unrewarded, I promise you that!"

Molly, who had had an eye on a slightly worn dress of Cecie's, brightened noticeably, but hastened to add, "That won't be needful, my lady. I do it for you without any of that."

"And I know you do," Cecie agreed. Then with a shrewd guess, she added, "But I thought you might just like that green morning dress, the one with the fringed skirt. It would be very becoming with your green eyes, you know. Do say you will take it."

Giggling, the maid nodded her agreement, and the dress in question was unearthed from the wardrobe that held it and carried away by the happy co-conspirator.

It was a much more solemn Molly who returned later that evening to find her mistress waiting for her in the bedroom.

"Well, did you ask him? What did he say?" Cecie asked before the door had been closed.

"I ask him, and he did answer me truthfully, Lady Cecie," Molly said without her usual smile.

Cecie's heart skipped a beat. "What is it, Molly? You must tell me, you must!"

Glancing around the room with apprehension, Molly gestured toward the window embrasure of the far side of the bed, well away from the door to the hall. The two young girls huddled there, shivering slightly with fear and excitement.

"Well? No one in the hall can hear us talking, although I can't imagine anyone trying to. Do tell me."

Molly, her face arranged in an expression of most solemn warning, hissed out her secret. "They do go to France, Lady Cecelia."

"Oh, dear." Despite her suspicions, Cecie was disappointed with this confirmation of Peter's lack of faith. Realizing the absurdity of this, she shook herself and pressed Molly's hand.

"What sort of a cargo do they carry, Molly? They are smuggling, aren't they?"

Now that the awful word was hanging in the air between them, Molly lost her reserve. "That

51

is just what they be doing! I gave Willie a piece of my mind, I can tell you. Him with a good, respectable job and fine prospects, looking to throw it all away with such foolishness." Here she stopped, overcome with her young man's lack of common sense and his alarming display of folly.

There was an angry gleam in Cecie's eyes as she sought to comfort the girl. "I fear that poor Willie is being led into this out of loyalty to Mr. Peter, Molly. Don't be too hard on him."

"Well, it's not my place to say anything about that, my lady, but Mr. Peter do have a crew of some of the handiest lads from hereabouts working with him. They been bringing in casks of brandy and wine and bolts of fine cloth, like what Mr. Peter give you the other day." Hearing her own words, Molly began to look at Cecie with dawning sympathy.

"I feared as much. Did Willie know when they were to go out next?"

"He say that they would wait for the darkest time of the month. The new moon will be first week in September. That make it easier for them to miss being seen by the revenue cutters, you see."

"Yes, I see it all too well. That is nearly two weeks off. You must make Willie tell you the exact night when they are leaving for France, Molly. I want to be able to do something to stop this foolishness, and I have a plan that I think will work, but I need to know when I can catch Mr. Peter red-handed."

Molly nodded eagerly. "I did tell him that he was to let us know as soon as word was out. You can count on Willie, my lady. He'll do it for you."

"You should say that he will do it for *you,* Molly. I am grateful for all the help you have given me. I intend to put a stop to this smuggling if I can. They are like little boys playing at being pirates. It is disgusting!"

Molly wasn't sure that she understood about pirates. Smugglers were one thing and pirates another, and she thought even less of the latter than she did of the first. But her young lady's resolve did much to comfort her and she was anxious to do what she could to help. Only one thing worried her more than the smuggling.

"Lady Cecie, I don't feel right, keeping the dress like this, what with all the bad news I brung you." She stroked the material of the gown wistfully, avoiding Cecie's eyes.

"Don't be silly. You must keep the dress and continue to wear it. You look very pretty in it. I insist! Now, is Mr. Peter still keeping his boat over in Bird Cove?"

"That he is. And I know a secret way to get there, one I can show you some day when they go out in the yacht for a quick sail."

"Good. I could not have chosen a better ally for this endeavor."

Molly bridled, then added, "My lady, there be one thing more you should hear of."

"What is this?"

"I weren't the first to be asking Willie about the *Mary Ann*."

Cecie stood very still, chilled by the danger implied in this news. "Who else was there?"

"The Major, he talked to Willie earlier this day. He were asking all the same questions."

Cecie frowned. "Oh, he was, was he? And just what did Willie tell him?"

Molly's grin was unexpected but encouraging. "Not a thing that would matter. He said that they often put into Plymouth, when the winds be right, and that sometime Mr. Peter would buy goods for his mother in the shops there and carry it back on the boat."

Cecie grinned too. "And did the Major accept this?"

"He seemed to, or so Willie say. And he weren't too pleased by half, I can tell you. My Willie, he say the Major walked away with a scowl on his face fit to scare the fish from the sea."

"Good." As long as Hugh failed to find any evidence of Peter's activities, Cecie thought she could use his interest in the affair to her own advantage in the coming confrontation. But it would never, never do for Armstrong to have more than vague suspicions. He and Peter had long been rivals, at least in the Major's eyes, and she suspected that he would be pleased to put Peter in the wrong, even place him in a dangerous situation if the opportunity arose. The affair was becoming very complicated, indeed.

54

"Then we must wait until September, Molly. There is little I can do until then. But I promise you that I will stop this smuggling once and for all!"

Six

Cecie spent the next two weeks striving for calm. The effort to remain natural in her behavior and countenance, unperturbed by the warring thoughts in her mind, was such that if she had met her cousin Peter, she would have overthrown her well considered plans and confronted him on the spot, regardless of the consequences to the young man and herself.

But she did not see her cousin Peter. He was always away, in Fowey or Plymouth or Falmouth, or visiting friends here, there and everywhere. If she had not known better, she would have suspected him of avoiding her. It was all so frustrating, but also comforting that the temptation to forget her clever ideas was removed so conveniently. She would proceed along the course of her carefully laid campaign, her well organized campaign, for that was the best chance she had of bringing Peter back to his senses. In any case, she found she must adhere to it whether she liked it or not.

On the other hand, Hugh Armstrong was always there. His manner toward her had become more conciliatory and he claimed as much of her time as he could, taking advantage of her instinctive courtesy toward a guest in her parents' house, a guest moreover who was closely connected with her family, for all his faults. With smiles and soft words, he sought to put himself on a friendly footing with the girl, while aiming occasional shafts at Peter's character. The niceties of his attentions were obvious to those around them, even her father taking notice, and Lord Penrith forgot his disappointment in Peter's unusual absences as he looked to Hugh with new thoughtfulness. Cecie tried to ignore the officer as much as she could, but her irritation occasionally rose to the surface, and her mocking tone should have warned him that his ploys were useless.

Her father's house was so near the sea that mists and fogs were the norm, not the exception. The frequent cloudy nights were another trial for her, for she could not check the progress of the moon. She knew in her mind that it was reducing itself to a sliver over the course of the nights, but her heart needed the reassurance of seeing it hanging in the sky. Every night she would peek out past her curtains, to show herself that all was proceding as it ought, and many nights she went to bed unsure. As the date of the new moon approached, the weather presented another sort of anxiety to the girl. What if it were to storm? Peter might change his plans from moment to moment, in such a way that her faithful spy, Molly's Willie, could not contact them in time. Then all would be lost, for she greatly feared that Peter's luck was running out. There was more and more talk of extra cutters guarding the coastline, the land riders had been reinforced in just the last days of August, and Hugh Armstrong kept postponing his return to London in a most alarming way.

The anxiety of her wait made Cecie even more restless than is usual for a young girl of seventeen, and she nearly drove her family to distraction. Lady Penrith even saw fit to banish her from the sewing room, her fidgeting was so irritating and disruptive. So Cecie took to her horse and wandered over the Cornish hills of her father's estate, frequently finding her way to the sea.

It was on one of these rides, only three days before she calculated the new moon, that she had been arguing with herself as she made her way toward the cove where Peter's boat was beached. She was trying to convince the demon within her to turn aside from that particular path, when she had a disturbing encounter with Major Armstrong. The man still lingered under her parents' roof, and he was mounted on a magnificent black stallion, known by Cecie to be a gift of her too generous father. The horse pranced and preened on the grass of the slope, showing off itself and its rider.

"Hey there, Cecie! Here you are!" Hugh pulled his mount up beside the girl's mare with a flurry of dirt and hooves. He stood up in his stirrups and swept her a bow, making a handsome figure on the beast he rode. The bright August sun played on his blond hair left bare by the removal of his hat.

Cecie barely returned the bow. "Major Armstrong."

"Come, come, now, Cecie, we have been friends too long for such formality," he said, laughing, then added, "or are you practicing for your London Season?"

"I am not practicing for anything at all," she said shortly.

"Then you must be angry with me. Have I disturbed your peace? I know that you have spent much time of late on these moors, riding without apparent aim. Or has it been for the purpose of working off excess energy and troublesome thoughts? I fear that I have interrupted you."

He smiled down at her from his superior height, his horse falling in with her mare's pace. "Not at all, sir."

"Sir? There it is again."

His bantering tone did little to soothe her disgruntled mind. "It is a lovely day for a ride. We are fortunate to have such fine weather at this time of year."

Realizing that his banter was going to be ignored rather than returned, he abandoned it with grace and took her lead. "Yes, the sun has done a wonderful job of burning off the usual fogs and mists that plague this dismal piece of country."

Cecie smiled for the first time and seized the opening he had given her. "Dismal? If you so dislike this part of the world, I am surprised that you cling to it so tenaciously."

She had miscalculated. "The company more than compensates me for an occasional morning of mist. At times, I even fancy that it adds to the romantic aura of the place, a thing that is not to be despised, don't you agree?"

She blushed and then looked out over the horizon to where the blue sea could be seen in the distance. Lifting her face, she felt the cool rush of the breeze off the water and was refreshed. "There appears to be a ground swell coming. I hope it does not foretell a storm."

He glanced over in the same direction, oblivious to the beauty of the sun and sea, and shrugged. "Yes, that could be all the worse for your cousin Peter, don't you think? It would put all his plans awry."

"In what way does this weather affect Peter?" she asked, her head still turned, only her back visible to him.

"He is soon to put out his boat, I hear."

She turned to him with sudden energy, then gained control of herself. "Oh? I had not heard so."

"But Cecie, you know as well as I that there will be no moon in but a few days' time. That will be the ideal time for his activities."

"No moon?"

"Yes, no moon. It will soon be one of the darkest nights of the month," he said with a hint of amusement in his expression, despite the solemn, gentle voice he was using.

"And whatever good would that do Peter? And what are the activities you make much of?" She was facing him squarely now, her horse having sidled around to enable her to do so with comfort, and for a moment their mounts were headed in opposite directions, although still side by side.

"His trading activities, my dear. Surely you knew? Everyone else about the district seems to be fully aware of it."

"And who told you that?"

"As I say, it is common knowledge, discussed in every taproom hereabouts. Several have told me of it."

Cecie found herself laughing with real mirth. She was sure now that Major Armstrong knew little of real value and was trying to discover what little information she was in possession of. The secrets of the Trade were well kept and would never be revealed to an outsider, especially in so public a place as an ale house.

"Then you are better informed than I, Major Armstrong. I hear no such talk. But then, I don't frequent vulgar haunts."

Armstrong's face flushed but he controlled his anger, "Oh. I could have sworn that you knew something and were this minute making your way to Bird Cove, where your cousin's boat is beached."

So the man did know something, but only what was common knowledge. "I have not made up my mind where I go. As you have already noted, I often ride without any object or destination beyond the joy of the fields and sea and sky. They suffice me quite well, you know."

"But there is little to see this way but Bird Cove," he answered too quickly, his vexation at her mockery showing in the set of his handsome mouth.

"On the contrary, there is the little chapel past the cove, and the Holy Well before it, either of which offers a pleasant view to the lonely rider. I find their solitary beauty refreshing."

Her displeasure with his company was becoming more and more obvious as her barbed tongue flicked through the courtesies of the conversation. He could not help but be stung and she wished it so.

"It is refreshment doubled in the sharing, I am sure," he said with determination.

"Really? I had not noticed it so."

The officer's patience suddenly snapped and an ugly look came over his face. "Stop this bantering, Cecie. You know as well as I that your beloved cousin Peter Pendyne is a smuggler, the leader of the Gentlemen of this district. There is no point in you trying to hide it from me."

"Peter, a smuggler?" She gazed at him with wide blue eyes radiating innocence and a hint of mirth. "If you know that to be true, it is your duty as a citizen to report him to the nearest magistrate or to some other authority. It is your duty as an officer of the King, making it a double burden."

"It is the duty of every loyal English man, and woman," he said with heavy meaning.

"Of course. But it is you who are making claims of such knowledge, not I. I have no proof that any laws have been broken."

"I don't believe you!"

She ignored him and pressed on. "And if I had such suspicions as you are voicing now, I would be wise enough to wait until I had found the proof to go with them before making wild accusations," she ended with a sniff.

Armstrong realized that he had done his cause more damage than good with this last exchange. "I do not wish to seem harsh as regards Peter, Cecie. I know how fond you are of him. I know that he stands in the position of a brother to you." Here he paused, a more tender look in his eyes. "It is for your sake that I hesitate to act. I don't wish to cause you any unhappiness. You are very dear to me."

"I know not why you say that. If you perceive that you are duty bound to perform a certain act, then it is dishonorable of you to shirk it, no matter what the cause."

Armstrong leaned over as if to hear her words better, then reached out his hand to touch her shoulder. Cecie jerked back so abruptly that her horse was startled and backed off a few paces. "I ask for your help in bringing Peter back to his senses. I feel sure that this is only a lark, a great adventure he has taken up for his own amusement, or perhaps as part of a wager. If he needed any money, he would have had the sense to apply to your father, as he has done in the past. Please try to understand my position. . . ." He had been sidling his mount toward her again, but this last off-handed accusation, that Peter had begged money from her father, was more than she could bear.

"Peter has been given an allowance by my father, as is proper, inasmuch as the title will one day be his. He has never asked for more than that, of this I am certain."

Armstrong contrived to look both pitying and amused at this declaration of faith, and once more reached out his hand. "Dearest Cecie, your loyalty does you honor, but there are things about your cousin of which you are ignorant. You must allow me to educate you in this."

"Thank you, no." He had nearly touched her again, an unpleasant smile on his lips, but she tightened her hold on her reins and spurred her mount into a gallop that carried her in the direction of home. Before Armstrong could get his horse swung about to follow, she had disappeared over a rise of hill and into a stand of trees.

It was that very night, when, her nerves stretched taut by the day's encounter, Molly told her that a time and date had been set for the smuggling venture. The yacht *Mary Ann* was to set sail on the next night, but two days before the moon was dark. Cecie felt only relief that the torment of her waiting was to end.

Seven

It was with her thoughts in a turmoil, no resolve quite firm enough, her suspicions nagging her at every turn, doubts rising up to haunt her, that she greeted the last day of August. The night before had been a sleepless one and her nerves were raw.

"Are you quite sure, Molly? He did say the thirty-first? Today? It is a day or so before the darkest day of the moon. Why are they leaving so early?"

Molly soothed her agitation as best she could. "It were the Captain's orders, Willie say."

"The Captain? Oh, you mean Mr. Peter."

"The crew, they call him Captain. It's fitting, seeing as how he captains the yacht."

"But why is he risking going out with a moon still shining? Perhaps he knows that he is being watched and is planning some sort of subterfuge."

"Well, I don't know what that be, my lady, but there won't be much of a moon to worry about tonight, just a sliver. Maybe he wants to allow time to put off the trip if something come up. This way he can wait as much as a week and still sail safely."

Cecie looked at her maid with a flash of laughter on her face. "You are far more sensible than I, Molly. These last few days have been a sad trial for me. All this waiting is wearing on one's patience. I should have thought of that myself."

"It be more than the waiting, my lady, what with Major Armstrong always about you the way he is," Molly answered, her partisan hackles rising. The maid's indignation was apparent but Cecie chose to shrug it off.

"He is after all a close connection, Molly, and a welcome guest in this house. My father enjoys his company."

"He never bothered this much before, Lady Cecilia." The warning was on two levels, but Cecie, with her own preoccupations, thought of only one.

"Yes, I fear he suspects Peter. But after tonight, I trust there will be nothing for him to see or discover."

On this note of firm resolve, Cecie made herself as comfortable as she could for her last difficult hours of patience.

On the afternoon of the thirty-first, Hugh was still in residence at Penrith Hall, making himself a charming and agreeable companion to Cecie's father and lavishing as much of his attention on the young lady of the house as he could arrange in the face of her open animosity. Lord Penrith, a man without guile or suspicion, accepted this renewal of his relationship with the younger man with pleasure; his wife considered the courtesies to their daughter overdone and unwelcome. The household had rubbed along together with tolerable good humor, and the visit was deemed a success by the two gentlemen involved, but Cecie's ill humor was barely concealed.

To Cecie, the time was standing still. She had explored her route to the cove, feeling sure that she would have no trouble finding her way in the dark. She had rehearsed the scene in her mind many times, when she would arrive at the *Mary Ann* and Peter would be confronted with the perfidy of his actions and warned of the danger he risked with Hugh Armstrong in the neighborhood, bruiting suspicions and nosing about. If neither of these arguments were enough to convince him to turn his back on the illegal enterprise, she would resort to pleading, an alternative that was painful but one which she would employ if she must. Somehow she would save Peter—and Willie and the others—from the foolish game they were playing. They were like little boys who, failing to perceive the danger of their pastime, were due for a scolding to set them to rights.

Supper that evening was made particularly trying by Hugh Armstrong's attentions. He sat next to her, too close for her comfort, pressing dishes and condiments on her. She had no desire to eat in the first place, her thoughts on the night's adventures ahead, and his insistence that she try the lobster, the pâté, this ragout of beef, some excellent mustard, was more than she could bear. Not even the sweets appealed to her, despite his lavish praise of the pastries and cakes that were served.

"Are you feeling unwell, Cecie?" her mother asked as the ladies departed for the drawing room to allow the gentlemen to indulge in port. "Your appetite is not at all what it should be and you look quite wan. Whatever can be the matter with you?"

"I am very well, Mama. Perhaps just a trifle tired these last days."

"You have been preocupied of late, child."

Cecie nodded her head. "I have much to tell Peter when he returns."

Lady Penrith drew her own conclusions from this admission. "And having a house guest while in the midst of these fittings has proven a trial, I suspect. It is so hard to play hostess when one's mind is on other things."

Cecie, who had paid little attention to either her gowns or the guest, was at a loss as to how to reply. "Perhaps it is just the heat," she murmured at length.

"We shall have to take better care of you. It would not do for you to look pale and worn before your Season has even begun. Although I suppose we could wait until next spring, if you wish. I had my heart set on showing you off this fall, you know, but that is a small matter. What do you think?"

"Fall? Spring? It does not make one whit of

difference to me, Mama," Cecie said in a rush before she realized the full horror of her words.

"Cecilia! You *are* unwell! This Season should be the most exciting event in your life! What has gone wrong, darling? Are you sure you do not have a fever?"

"No, Mama. I am perfectly well. I spoke in haste. Please forgive my ill-considered words. They meant nothing."

"Let me feel your forehead."

"No! Please, it is nothing." By now Cecie was nearly in tears, and her mother withdrew her hand, fearing to upset the girl even more. Wiser than her lord and husband, an inkling of suspicion had crept into the lady's mind and she was suddenly sure that she had a full understanding of the case.

"Of course not, Cecie. You are perfectly fine, I am sure. Such a silly fuss over nothing." Her smile was sympathetic and reassuring as she continued her comfort. "I went through a similar confusion when I met your father, dear. There were so many things happening to me that were new and unfamiliar that I did not know what to think. It will pass with time."

"Confusion? What does Papa have to do with it?"

Her mother only smiled again. "You wait and see. Your old friend will be back in the neighborhood in a week or two, and you will find ease in his companionship, I am sure. Mrs. Pendyne has assured me that Peter will return by mid-September. Then we will be quite on our old

71

footing with Pendyne Manor, and you two children will be able to see one another again."

Cecie had no idea what her mother was talking about and could only shake her head with confusion. The sound of the gentlemen approaching the drawing room warned them that their tête-à-tête was soon to end.

"Mama, would it be terribly rude of me if I were to go up early this evening? I feel rather more tired than usual."

Lady Penrith, hearing the major's voice, smiled and nodded her permission to this plan. "It would be more restful for all of us, I think."

Cecie lingered only long enough to wish her father and the guest a good night, then hurried off to her room. When Lord Penrith turned to his wife with a look of concern, she patted his hand and whispered, "There are great things afoot for Cecie. I will tell you about it later," and turning her attention, she set about entertaining their persistent visitor.

Eight

Cecie crept out from behind the large boulder that had given her its shelter. Peter's yacht, rocking gently in the calm of the protected water, was anchored near the arm of rocks that formed the breakwater for the cove. Low tide had just turned and she could see a stony pathway leading from the shore along the rocks of the breakwater to the prow of the boat. No one was about, as nearly as she could tell, but she took the precaution of wrapping more tightly around her the worn brown riding habit she had donned for this adventure.

It had been easy to slip out of the house with Molly's help, her parents and Hugh Armstrong occupied with their own talk after dinner. She had found her way over the headland without difficulty, the dim white of the abandoned crosses marking the path for her, and from her present vantage point she could see the whole of the cove. Two stubborn arms of rock thrust out into the rough waters of the English Channel, breaking the current's strength and providing a pool of calm that lapped a narrow, sandy beach. The back of the cove rose into rocky cliff, and footholds were treacherous on its face, but for those who knew their way, the going was easy enough and safe; many Cornish miners served as occasional tubmen for the smugglers and knew their way quite well, indeed. In the dim light of the stars, showing solid masses of immovable shadow in the glitter of the water's surface broken by lines of froth brought in by the waves, it was hard to believe that anything nefarious was afoot. Directly to the south was the Channel, patrolled by the navy and the coast guard vessels, to the left, eastward, was Dodman Point. At a greater distance down the coast in the other direction, where the land lowered to the southwest, was the mouth of the River Fal and the naval station of Falmouth. The rocks and hills behind, the sea breeze in one's face, all was as it had been for generations of Cornish people.

And to the east and south was France.

Cecie peered around her one last time before leaving the shadows. There was something missing from the cove, some integral part of its character. Then she realized that the great noisy flocks of seabirds that scavenged the beach during the day were silent in the dark. She had never before been to the cove after nightfall, and the absence of their sound cast an eerie pall on her spirits difficult to ignore.

Moving with great caution, she went toward

the stretch of rocks that jutted into the black water, another shadow that was solid, like the rocks, yet moving and heaving. Her path was still slippery and damp from the waves of the receding tide that had washed over it, and Cecie could see that the water was already beginning to creep back to claim its own. She avoided clumps of seaweed and ankle-twisting crevices as best she could in the faint starlight, but despite her care she still stumbled and fell several times, cutting herself painfully. She estimated that Peter would be hoisting anchor with the floodtide, and that the one place he would have to face her with shame was aboard his own smuggling vessel. She was determined to argue him away from the course he had charted.

Sooner than she had expected, the side of the boat loomed beside her. Once to her goal, she gathered her skirts tightly about her and jumped as far as she could, timing her leap for the rocking deck, trying to reach it when the ship was tilted to face her. Luck was with her, sending a little wash of water to move the boat closer to her perch, and she found herself landing with a bone-wrenching thud on the deck. In a flash she had reached the deep shadows cast by the pile of nets that filled the deck. Still, no alarm had been raised.

Cecie had lived near the coast all her life and moved around boats, even this unfamiliar one, with ease. It was a small matter for her to discover the hatchway to the cabin and let herself down the narrow ladder to the passageway leading to her goal. In the dark she collected a few more scrapes and bruises, but these failed to daunt her. She was nearly through with her mission, now all that was left was to wait for Peter. She felt the tension that had carried her through the nerve-racking days and sleepless nights draining from her.

The cabin she found was a Spartan affair, furnished with only a chair and the built-in bunk of the bulkhead. She groped around in the dark and settled on the bunk as the more comfortable of the two choices, the chair being a rickety one, an unfortunate characteristic for anything subject to unexpected shipboard motion. Curling up on the rough blanket that covered the bed, she shivered slightly in her damp, soiled clothes.

The water slapped against the side of the boat in a slow, lulling pattern. With the blanket clutched about her, Cecie found herself warm and comfortable. Her wait didn't look to be too unpleasant an experience, snug in the yacht's cabin as she was. She sent up a prayer of thanks for this small blessing and leaned against the bolster at the head of the bed.

No sooner had she put her cheek to it, she fell into the deep, untroubled sleep of an innocent child who has had a long, tiring day. No sound would disturb her.

The crew approached the vessel nearly an hour later, creeping cautiously along the beach to the dories they had hidden among the rocks. Soon the water would have risen sufficiently for the hull of the boat to clear the treacherous entrance of the cove. The coast guard was known to be out that night, and every precaution was used to assure that no attention focused on Bird Cove. The watchman, who had dozed contentedly with his bottle of rum on a rock above the path Cecie had taken, checked men by with officious care, muttering to each under his breath and waving his pistol until he had seen the face of the man. The last to arrive was Peter Pendyne, leader of the enterprise and captain and owner of the vessel being used. With a grin and a flash of his own pistol, he squelched the pomposity of the watch.

"Has there been any unusual activity, Jeb?" he asked in a low voice.

The grizzled fisherman shook his head with self righteous vigor. "Nary a breeze to ruffle the waves, sur."

"Any activity out in the Channel? You did keep an eye peeled on the sea, didn't you? The coast guard cutters aren't likely to come into the cove, you know. It's much better from their point of view to catch us in the open water. Makes for more damning evidence in court."

His cohort laughed through his grizzled beard, sending a waft of alcohol-ladened breath into Pendyne's face. "Hardly that, Cap'n Pendyne. I knows me business. Beside, they need to find a cargo of brandy in her hold afore they can make their charges." And with his courage stiffened by a pint of rum, the old man really believed it.

Pendyne was more skeptical, but he had other

77

means of checking the activity in the area and accepted the man's assurances with a shrug. "That had better be true, Jeb, or we'll pay dearly for this night's work."

The old man cackled even louder, ignoring the secrecy he had entertained before. "There ain't no chance of that, Cap'n, not with you at the helm. You be the luckiest smuggler in the history of Cornwall, and that say a lot, that do."

The younger man acknowledged the compliment with a grim smile, ignoring the smell of rum that still filled the air between him and the sailor. "Then we had best set about it, Jeb. Tonight will be an important one for us."

The two set out for the last of the dories, Pendyne in the lead. Slipping and sliding on the wet stones in the dark, they were relieved when they arrived at the small boat. The path along the arm of rocks had long since been covered with water at its beach end. On a night as dark as this one, being at sea with the stars to guide them was safer than the uncertainty of the rocky land they had turned their backs to.

The ship was soon out of the calm waters of the cove, moving swiftly and silently toward the French coast. Peter Pendyne, unaware that he carried an extra cargo in his cabin, looked toward the Continent with rising spirits. This *was* to be an important night for all of them, something he knew more about than any of his crew, but he kept his thoughts to himself. He spent the last hours of the night on deck, directing his men in their work.

*   *   *

It was nearly dawn when the *Mary Ann* sighted the mouth of the inlet that was her destination. As the light of the sun began to streak the sky over the chalky cliffs, the young sailor standing watch gave a shout of warning. "Ship to starboard!"

All hands turned to stare at the intruder. Pendyne grabbed his spyglass and directed it at the flag of the war sloop that was fast bearing down on his smaller craft. "English, men. We'll have to make a run for the creek. They are running out their guns."

The men turned to their tasks with practiced speed, racing up the mast and handling the lines with skill and efficiency. A puff of smoke could be seen floating from the prow of the advancing sloop, followed by the roar of the gun and the splash of a cannonball that had passed over the stern of the *Mary Ann*. Jeb, his bottle of rum long since empty, ducked his head and whimpered near the mast.

"Get to it, man. You are only making matters the worse by not doing your job. Get up that mast, you blockhead, and help them give me all the sheet we can muster. We are going to have a close race of it."

Jeb didn't dare reply. The calm good sense of his captain's orders somehow penetrated his foggy brain and he shambled over to the mast and began pulling his share of line as best he could. Pendyne stared after him with a wry grin on his face, then turned to face the sloop.

79

The race was even closer than he had expected. The strongly armed ship bore down on the *Mary Ann* with a graceful speed that struck his jaundiced eye as diabolically unfair. As the small yacht entered the mouth of the inlet and the safety it represented, the sloop changed tack, presenting a broadside, guns primed and ready, to the hapless vessel. With a casual sweep past the calm waters of the river's mouth, she loosed a devastating salvo on the smugglers, shattering their mast and sending shot into the wooden hull, just below the waterline. The *Mary Ann* limped into the safety of the creek, losing sight of her attacker behind the friendly cliffs of the coast. With maniacal determination, the crew and its captain managed to steer her to a small beach near where they had planned to anchor her. There, she was beached.

Out in the Baie de la Seine, the sloop veered off, tacking north. The appearance of two frigates from the direction of Havre de Grâce explained the sudden loss of interest.

The attack did not result in any deaths among the crew, although several were injured. One young boy had fallen from the mast and been knocked unconscious on the deck, two men were struck by flying splinters thrown up by the impact of the shot in the deck, and another had suffered a broken leg when the mast fell. Jeb scraped his arm against the rough wood of the deck and complained bitterly of this ill usage, but few heeded him.

In the cabin below, Cecie, awakened from a

deep sleep by the first sound of gunfire, had tried somewhat groggily to determine where she was and how she had come to be there. She had been thrown against the bulkhead of the cabin as she rose from the bunk when the patrol ship's broadside had shaken the *Mary Ann*. She lay on the cabin floor unconscious, the blood dripping from a gash in her forehead, to be found soon by a frightened sailor.

Nine

Peter tenderly carried Cecie in his arms all the way to the small inn of the village outside of Courseulles. She was bleeding only slightly and by the time he had placed her in the best bed the inn could offer, a bruise and a scab were all the evidence of her injury, discounting her pallor and closed eyes. He bathed away the streaks of blood and dirt, cursing all the while under his breath against the fate and the day he'd been born. The wife of the inn's owner, a sleazy woman with blown hair and a fat, rolling figure, was not permitted to touch the girl, but Peter feared that he would have to seek out some woman of good repute to aid him with her nursing. He was debating this course with himself when the still figure showed her first signs of life.

Cecie stirred only slightly, but it was enough to set Peter's heart beating with hope. His gentle touch on her forehead, where he had been placing a damp cloth at intervals, caused her to swat at his arm feebly, and the next moment her eyes were opening.

"Peter, wherever am I?" was the first thing she thought to say. She barely moved, but was able to glance around the strange room with an alarm heightened by her pain and confused mental state.

"Cecie, thank God you are still alive! When the man told me that there was an injured girl in the cabin, and I saw it was you, I was beside myself with worry. What in the world were you doing there, love? You could have been even more seriously hurt or even killed if the British ship had been more thorough in her work."

"Where am I?" She had ignored most of his diatribe and clung to the point that was frightening her. She had thought she knew all the homes and inns in the area of her father's country estate, at least so that she could guess the locale from a glance out the window. But by painfully propping herself up on one elbow, she saw only a strange view through the rough curtains.

"You are in France!" Peter was impatient with her preoccupation with the obvious. "Surely you were aware that we were crossing the Channel? Where else could we be?"

She had *not* been aware. "France? How could that be? I went to the *Mary Ann* for the express purpose of preventing you from continuing your smuggling, Peter. I was going to stop you from this foolish trip. How could you have managed to do such a thing?"

"I had no idea you were on my boat, that is

how I managed it. Do you think I would have put out if I had known that you were skulking in my cabin?"

"I was not skulking! I had slipped on board to confront you in such a way that you would be forced to confess that you had not kept faith with me, so that you would see the full danger of what you were doing. I was going to warn you that you are in the gravest danger of being discovered, discovered by someone who would have no compunction about turning you over to the authorities."

"I know about Armstrong, damn it, Cecie. Why in the world didn't you show yourself if you had such fine plans for an argument? It would have saved you this trip to France."

Cecie stared at him for a moment, then confessed in a tiny voice. "I fell asleep."

Peter could only bury his face in his hands. At first Cecie feared that he was very angry with her, but then the sight of his shaking shoulders warned her that it was much worse than that: he was laughing.

"Peter, how dare you laugh at me like this! This is not a laughing matter! This is serious!"

He shook his head, raising it to reveal tears in his eyes, tears of uncontrolled amusement. "I know how serious it is, Cecie, far more than you do. You have put my enterprise in the gravest jeopardy! What am I going to do?"

"I *meant* to put your enterprise in jeopardy. I meant to put an end to it. So there." She tried to flounce, no mean feat when lying in a dizzy state on a lumpy mattress, and only succeeded in jarring her sore head.

"We must get you back to England, but how?"

"Why, on the *Mary Ann,* of course!"

"That cannot be, Cecie." He was very sober when he gave her this answer, something she had not expected, and she felt a rising alarm.

"Of course you can."

"She was too badly damaged by the guns of that war sloop. It will be nearly a week before she will be able to put to sea."

"Then find me another passage!"

"How? England and France are at war with one another. We all stand in danger of being arrested and thrown into prison as enemy aliens. We are in a devilish predicament, Cecie!"

"Prison?" Now she was really frightened. "None of this would have happened if you had kept your word to me."

"Let's not go back to that tale again. It may surprise you to know that I have kept my word. Cecie, you are going to have to do exactly what I tell you to if we are to get out of this mess unharmed."

"I will not! I do not trust you, Peter, and furthermore. . . ."

The sound of a knock at the door of the room silenced her. She looked at the wooden panels, then at Peter, then lay back on the bed and pulled the coarse blanket up to her nose. Peter, with a gesture of silence, rose to open the door.

Standing in the hall was an officer of the

French army, a Captain, in a uniform impressive from the cockade in his hat to the shine of his boots. "Monsieur Pendyne?" His pronunciation of the English name was a trifle hesitant.

"Oui, monsieur le capitaine," Peter answered in fluent French, the language that he was to use for the most part in the next few days. At the sound of his native tongue being spoken so clearly, the officer smiled and was cordial.

"It is an honor to greet you in the name of Minister Count Talleyrand and the Imperial government, monsieur. I am Captain Duval and I have been assigned the task of escorting you."

"Escorting me?"

"Yes. Count Talleyrand has requested that you journey back to Paris and meet him there. He is most anxious to speak to you in person, Monsieur Pendyne."

Peter suddenly remembered that the conversation was being conducted in the hall of a public inn and courteously gestured to the Frenchman to enter the room. The captain did so, casting a curious glance in Cecie's direction and then ignoring her presence with elaborate nonchalance.

"I am honored with this unexpected invitation," Peter said with every show of cordiality. "I had hoped for such an opportunity, having heard of the minister's excellent reputation, but I had not thought to be so fortunate."

"The minister is most anxious to see you, too, Monsieur Pendyne," the captain agreed, parrot-fashion, pleased that his task was proving so easy. He had orders to get this Englishman to Paris, one way or the other, as he suspected the other man was well aware.

A sudden motion from the bed reminded Peter that Cecie, with her excellent command of French, was undoubtedly following the whole conversation and had to be accounted for. He knew that the Frenchman had already drawn his own conclusions about the girl's presence, but feared that they would put his cousin on a difficult footing in a foreign land, a very difficult footing indeed for a young, innocent girl.

"I fear that my own plans have been somewhat disarranged, monsieur le capitaine," he said with a rueful gesture of his hands.

"Ah, the encounter with the British squadron was unfortunate. You have my sincerest sympathy there. But it will serve the purpose of making it more convenient for you to spend the next few days in our capital, Monsieur Pendyne. You would have had to wait in any case for the repairs to your yacht, repairs that will take some few days before the vessel can be afloat."

"That is something that I had expected to happen one day, as any sensible man would. The unexpected has also occurred." Here he paused to nod in Cecie's direction before continuing. "The young lady saw fit to stow away on board my boat." Cecie began to struggle into an upright position.

The captain smiled broadly. "Ah, yes, an affair of the heart. We Frenchmen understand such things."

"I would it were as simple as that."

"No? The young lady is married?"

"No, the young lady is my sister."

The look of disbelief said more than mere words could. Decent men do not expose their womenfolk to the dangers of the open sea—well, the Channel, anyway. They most especially do not do this in times of war. To expect a man of the world such as the captain to accept such a tale was insulting. And, if it were true, the Frenchman's sense of propriety was offended. He stared at Peter haughtily, not bothering to make a reply.

Then Cecie untangled her feet from the blanket and stalked over to Peter's side. "Peter, what are you doing? This is crazy. Tell this man to see to a boat that will take me back to England." Her tirade was delivered in quick English, too quick for the officer, Peter judged.

"Shush, Cecie. You must follow my lead."

But the sight of that angry face, blue eyes glaring up into matching blue eyes, the same determined chin thrust out, red curls quivering with indignation, carried the day. From being supercilious, the captain became confused, then reverted to his earlier obsequious courtesy.

"But of course, Monsieur Pendyne. It is all so very plain. But how did mademoiselle happen to be on board your ship?"

Peter dispelled any lingering suspicion with a grin that spoke much of masculine incomprehension in the face of feminine whim. "It was a prank."

"A prank? A very dangerous one, it would seem." Duval looked at Cecie sternly, seeking to impress on her his disapproval of such foolishness.

"Very dangerous. I was just remonstrating with her when you arrived, Captain." Peter smiled again with all the charm at his disposal and added. "Perhaps I can prevail upon you to come to my aid? I very much wish to return my sister to England before her absence arouses a general inquiry, for reasons that are obvious to you, I am sure. Can you help me find a boat that will carry her back?"

The captain thought this over, then shrugged his shoulders. "I am afraid that my briefing does not cover this possibility."

"Of course not. It was not expected. But it would seem the simplest solution to a difficult problem. I am sure that I can rely on her discretion to leave certain matters, ah, shall we say, confidential? This is of the utmost importance to me and to Minister Talleyrand."

The soldier refused to be persuaded. "My orders are only to take you to the minister in Paris. I cannot exceed them with such an action."

"But surely you see the sense of it?" Peter said with a flash of impatience. "If she is gone long from home there will be all sorts of people asking questions, questions that will help no one, least of all the minister."

The captain had suddenly made up his mind.

"No. We all, the three of us, shall leave for Paris in an hour. You will be able to supervise your sister in this way, as is only proper. It would not do to leave her in this inn, she is far too young and pretty."

"But she has sustained an injury while on board my yacht. When the British gunned us she was thrown against a bulkhead. She is not fit to travel."

The captain lost his patience. "One moment you would send her back to England, across seas infested with British ships, the next you say she cannot travel! We will leave within the hour."

Peter knew when he was beaten. "Very well, Captain Duval. We shall leave at your command."

Ten

Throughout this exchange, Cecie had been kept silent only by her fear. Despite her anger with Peter, she realized that he was her only hope for returning safely to her home and parents, and she appreciated that he was trying to get the French officer's help with just that project. When the door shut behind the Frenchman, she turned to Peter with despair.

"What is to happen to me?"

Peter's face was set in grim lines. "It would appear that you are to accompany me to Paris, in the very courteous custody of Captain Duval."

"Oh, Peter! No! That would just make it all the worse! I don't care what that man says, you can't let him do it."

"We have little choice, Cuz. Even if the captain were to relent and let you stay here, it is highly unlikely that I could find passage for you to England in such a short time. And he is right when he says that you cannot stay here alone.

It would be the height of folly to allow that."

"It would be the height of folly to take me to Paris," she said with a stamp of her foot.

"It was the height of folly to sneak aboard the boat, Cecie, as well you know. We shall have to make the best of the situation and that is final."

"Peter!"

"We must submit, for the simple reason that we have no choice. And that means that you must help me with this. Our resemblance has done much to convince the man that we are brother and sister. That may be the only thing that will provide you with my protection for the next few days. He could have as easily decided to leave you here to your own devices."

"Peter!"

"It is not to be thought of, Cecie! You are a young girl in a small French village. To stay without masculine protection? Absurd!"

"Couldn't Willie help me?"

He turned to her with impatience. "Listen to reason. You are a very pretty young girl, and the protection of a man with no standing, such as Willie, would do you little good."

"And you have standing?"

"Of a sort," he confessed, looking at her without flinching.

"Then I will do what I must." She turned away from him and walked toward the bed, leaning over it to straighten the blanket.

By so doing she missed the look of pain that crossed her cousin's face when he saw her sullen submission. That she did not trust him was obvious. "I will do all in my power to get you safely home," he promised.

"Then I am lucky, indeed. You seem to have a great deal of power around here."

"Cecie!"

"The great Talleyrand wishes to meet you. You will have his ear for whatever it is you have discovered. I am sure that he will gladly help you on this small matter of getting rid of a bothersome young girl."

"I do not have Talleyrand's ear. He doesn't trust me at all, as you would realize if you thought about it. That captain was ordered to get me to Paris, whether I wanted to go or not. We are both his prisoners."

She still refused to face him. "Of course. If you say so, Peter."

"Cecie, look at me."

There was something in his voice that made her turn around. "Just think of this, Peter. You will never be able to see England again, never. You have made yourself an outlaw with this smuggling, and now you are going to make it worse by collaborating with the French. You are an exile, without a country. The French will never really trust you, no matter how often they make use of you. You can never go home again."

She said all this with the utmost conviction and Peter was touched despite himself. "I only wish that you could know the whole of it, Cuz. I would dearly like to tell you all, but now is not the time or the place."

"I think I already know quite enough, thank

95

you. Your greed has led you to this, or perhaps it was only your senseless desire for adventure. But in any case there is no turning back."

"On that last we can agree. But in the future we must be careful of how we speak to one another, even in English. I doubt that the captain or anyone else here could understand us, but we can't be sure of that. From now on we shall have to assume that we are surrounded by spies, spies who will record every word we utter. Do you understand me?"

She looked at him with level eyes that showed no expression. "I understand."

"And you must help me, Cecie, for your own sake."

"I suppose."

Her indifference made him anxious. "You must play your part and play it well, if you expect to see England again, Cuz."

"Then I will do what I must."

In less than an hour, an hour that had passed in silence for the cousins after this last exchange, they were in a post chaise and on the road to Paris, no one bothering with the niceties of conversation.

The journey to Paris was an extremely fast one, with military horses waiting for them at the posting stops. Cecie, her head aching abominably, saw little of the passing countryside. She soon relented toward Peter to the extent of letting him put his arm around her to give her some protection from the jolting of the chaise;

rather he than the captain, who was eyeing her with more and more interest. She fell into blessed sleep after three hours on the road and a light lunch, oblivious in her exhaustion to the horrid jolts and musty interior of the carriage, although sometimes the former were too great and jarred her half awake.

Peter, who had after all not slept the night before, stared with stony eyes out the small window of the coach. He was careful to treat the officer with perfect courtesy, for given the position they were in that was imperative, but he was too exhausted for more. His tired mind told him that he must think, plan for the coming meeting with Count Talleyrand. Everything hinged on it. But he could barely keep himself awake and on more than one occasion found himself dozing against the top of Cecie's head, rubbing his cheek against her flaming curls. He was unaware of it, but they made a handsome couple, a picture that only the captain was there to admire.

The captain, sensible man that he was, was admiring only half of it. The young English girl was certainly delectable, but he sadly recognized that whatever her pranks and fits of foolishness, her brother was going to keep a strict eye on her, making closer acquaintance impossible. Not that it was proper for a mere captain to approach people of such great, if questionable, importance. He wasn't sure if Monsieur Pendyne was in truth an honored guest, as he had been instructed to treat him, or a prisoner, for he had also been told to do whatever was necessary to get him to Paris quickly. It was much safer to concentrate on seeing his duty done, much safer. He fingered his black pencil-thin moustache appreciatively, dreaming of the day when he would be far more than a mere captain and many girls such as mademoiselle would be his for the asking.

Meanwhile, his duty was being done with commendable efficiency. The post horses carried the chaise along the highways of France with great speed, and they were traveling much faster than mere civilians could ever hope to go. They would make excellent time to Paris, and then monsieur le capitaine Duval would present to Minister Talleyrand this monsieur Pendyne, and he supposed the sister, also; his duty would be discharged.

It was pitch dark when they pulled into Paris. The captain himself had no idea of the exact hour, and the Pendynes awoke in confusion and discomfort. The coach rumbled along the cobbled streets, drawing up finally at a house used by the government for visitors such as these. Cecie and Peter were escorted to the door, then shown their rooms with exquisite courtesy, all three ignoring the fact that there were armed guards patrolling the courtyard and standing at the front door. For the moment, Monsieur and Mlle. Pendyne were honored guests.

Captain Duval left them to catch what sleep

they could, warning Peter that he, Duval, would return for them early in the morning to escort them to an interview with Talleyrand. And on this cheerful note, he wished them good night.

Eleven

When Captain Duval arrived to escort them to their interview with Count Talleyrand, they were arguing. His presence enforced an uneasy silence on the young couple, but the fight continued none the less, intensified by their inability to voice it.

The carriage sent for them was a splendid affair, dark blue on the outside with red wheels, decorated with a coat of arms on the doors, later discovered to be that of the minister himself, and furnished on the inside with the softest plush and the most glittering gilt. Four horses pulled it and their trip was the most luxurious Cecie had ever enjoyed. This did little to soothe her conscience.

Peter had not wanted Cecie to accompany him in the first place, which was one of the causes for their early morning disagreement. He had even gone so far as to point out that she had only her shabby old riding habit to wear. She had felt that her presence and some special pleading from her own lips would convince the minister that she really ought to be sent home at the earliest opportunity. Peter, who had more detailed information about the character and interests of Monsieur Talleyrand, an undoubtedly brilliant diplomat but also an apostate bishop who had been forced to marry his current mistress by a disapproving Napoleon, had his doubts. The question was settled by Captain Duval, who had already reported Mademoiselle's presence to his superior and been instructed to bring her along. So along she came, ensconced in the most wonderful carriage she had ever seen, rolling through the streets of the city that many felt to be the most wonderful in the world. If she hadn't been so angry with Peter, and if the French had been the ally of her own beloved nation instead of the bitter enemy, she would have been enjoying herself immensely.

The suite of rooms to which they were taken looked as unlike government offices as Cecie could imagine. The furnishings were mostly of mahogany, all gilted in bronze, with an Egyptian motif predominant in the curved, scrolled lines, sphinxes, and figures in the dress of that race. The chair she was ushered to was upholstered in yellow silk shot silver and was far more comfortable than any she had sat in before, including her mother's prized winged-back chairs. The third chair in the room was even more wonderful than the ones she and Peter occupied, looking for all the world like a throne with its sky blue velvet and gold gilt mounts. The heavy drapery behind it, embroidered all over with bees, formed a frame for its glory, and without realizing it, Cecie's expectations of the chair's occupant adjusted suitably to this style.

The first sight of Charles-Maurice de Talley-rand-Périgord was something of a disappointment. He was slightly made, dressed in the height of fashionable elegance, undoubtedly rather old from the point of view of so young a girl, and he limped. True, it was a very graceful limp, and his cane was a beautiful one, but he did limp. Cecie had expected someone far more regal than this handsomely appointed gentleman with such an obvious physical defect, then was ashamed of herself for being prejudiced.

All such thoughts fled from her mind when the gentleman was standing there before her, leaning gracefully over her hand and kissing it. The most eloquent French rolled from his lips and without realizing it, she was being flattered by one of the most experienced lovers in France.

"Mlle. Pendyne, I am so honored to have this pleasure of meeting you. You brighten my poor, drab office with your charm and beauty." The words were simple enough, almost conventional in their compliments, but the manner in which he said them and glanced over her figure and face told her far more than mere sentences ever could. She was young enough to believe with all her heart that this sophisticated man of the world found her enormously attractive, that his compliments were heartfelt, and that he knew

103

of what he spoke. She was woman enough to want it so. It was only the scowling face of her cousin, seen over the satin shoulder of Monsieur Talleyrand, that brought her back to reality with a thud. Her smile became a nervous one and she retrieved her hand from the Frenchman's lips with a shy timidity, not a word escaping her mouth. A faint smile on the minister's face suggested that he had sensed her discomfort, and its source, and found both amusing.

"And Monsieur Pendyne. Such a pleasant surprise to finally meet you after these months of correspondence." He had turned to Peter and swept him a bow, one that the younger man barely returned, for the expression on Cecie's face had turned to one of angry disapproval at the discovery of his long connection with the French. "I trust that this visit to Paris will prove a pleasant one for you. I had no wish to inconvenience you, but of course, there are times when business must be discussed face to face, don't you agree?"

Peter murmured some vague sort of reply, whether to the first part of the statement or the latter it was not certain. Fortunately, Talleyrand was too much of a diplomat to care. He had the man Pendyne in his own offices, had fetched him there with a minimum of fuss, and had ordered everything to suit himself. He had little cause for complaint as he took his seat.

"But first we must make arrangements for Mademoiselle your sister."

"Yes, she must be sent back to England as quickly as possible," Peter said with relief.

"Of course. Every effort will be made to make Mademoiselle comfortable, I promise you." He had turned to face Cecie again. "I have been told that you speak some French, Mlle. Pendyne. It is most pleasing to me that such a lovely young lady would have command of our language, although if you would rather not indulge an old man, we can carry on the discussion in English."

"Oh, no, Monsieur le Ministre. I am quite conversable in French and would enjoy the opportunity to hear it spoken by such a distinguished diplomat." She was not looking at Peter as she spoke, and for the moment it seemed that she had forgotten his disapproving presence.

"Excellent, Mademoiselle. You are even more charming for your delicate flattery. Every Frenchman loves his language and feels that it is the most beautiful in the world. To have a beautiful woman such as yourself wish to hear it is the highest of compliments."

He would have said more in this vein, had not Peter, impatient with the flowery phrases and anxious to remove Cecie from the man's presence, broken in. "When will you be able to arrange for her passage, Count?"

The minister glanced at him with a charming smile. "I cannot tell you the precise hour, I fear. I have told Captain Duval to begin investigating possible means of transportation for the young lady."

Cecie interrupted. "Oh, good. Then I will get home soon?"

"Very soon, my dear, very soon." Talleyrand was once again smiling at her, his eyes lingering over the gentle swell of her bodice.

"Then she will be ready to leave on the instant," Peter said.

"Oh, hardly that."

"But you said. . . ."

"The French government would not consider sending so young and lovely a girl on a dangerous journey without taking every precaution to assure her safety and comfort. It may be several weeks before suitable passage can be arranged. I am sure that your brother will agree with me that all care must be taken in this matter." He was glancing from one to the other now, weighing their reactions to his statement.

"But I must get home immediately! I can't wait that long!" Cecie protested, near tears.

"It is quite impossible for her to remain in France," Peter added at the same time.

"It is quite impossible for her to do anything else, I fear." There was no hint of impatience in the man's voice, just amiable good will and friendly concern. "Every effort will be made to make Mademoiselle feel comfortable during her stay in Paris. As a matter of fact, I have arranged for her, and of course for you, too, Monsieur Pendyne, to have the use of a mansion in the finest residential district of the capital for the stay."

"A mansion?" Peter asked with horror. Little Cecie rattling around in a mansion? his face seemed to say.

"Yes, but of course. It is necessary that suitable quarters be provided for both of you. Your sister's presence merely adds to my desire to see you comfortably established."

"I had hoped that my sojourn in Paris would be brief and discreet, sir," Peter answered. "In fact, in view of the inability of Captain Duval to discover any quicker passage for my sister, I feel that I should return to the coast and hurry the repairs on my own yacht. I will be able to escort her to Cornwall myself in a few days, if all goes well."

"Ah, but your presence here in Paris is vital to us."

"How so? I am merely another Englishman, a foreigner."

"You underrate yourself, my dear sir, truly you do. You are considered a most important source of information. A vital source, in fact."

"You exaggerate my importance, Monsieur Talleyrand."

"Not at all, not at all. And it is not only I who deem you so." There was a significant pause while he looked from one youngster to the other, watching the question on their faces. Who other than Talleyrand would make such a decision?

"The Emperor himself is anxious to consult

with you. We will make it well worth your while."

"That is not part of the bargain!"

"No, it is not. I regret that it is necessary, but the situation has changed. Such is the way of the world, and only to be expected."

"This will expose me to the scrutiny of my own government, destroying my usefulness to you in the future. It will brand me a traitor."

Cecie had been following the argument with growing impatience, but this declaration stilled her. A traitor? She had thrown the possibility in his face, but this was the first time that the harsh word had been spoken.

"Peter, that is exactly what I feared!" she said in English. A look of annoyance crossed Talleyrand's face as he tried to sort through the foreign words.

"Careful, love. Use French. It would seem that I should have listened to you all along."

"Oh, Peter."

"I trust that this will not be an impossible hurdle to cross, Monsieur Pendyne. With our help, some tale will be concocted that will leave your reputation and usefulness intact. Rest assured that we will do everything in our power to aid a valuable agent."

His reassurances met with a cold silence. The two cousins exchanged looks of wary understanding. Peter was to help the French whether he wanted to or not. This threat, more than anything else could have done, was causing them to close family ranks.

"While you are in Paris, the Emperor wishes

you to be welcomed into French Society. I have arranged for a luncheon invitation or two for Mlle. Pendyne, to give her an opportunity to meet some ladies and make acquaintances before the grand court ball. And of course the dressmakers are hard at work creating costumes suitable for such a beautiful young lady's debut."

"Debut?" Cecie felt weak with fear. Too much was happening all at once, as if in a never never land of make believe.

"What ball?" from Peter.

"The one that will take place in but a few days. The Emperor is most insistent that the two of you be present."

"But that will make it impossible for us to regain faith when we return to England!" Cecie protested.

"Not at all. As I have told you, the French government is not without its resources in such matters. You must not worry so, dear child. Just enjoy your good fortune. It is not every English girl who can boast that she has waltzed with the Emperor of the French."

"I should say not!"

"My secretary has compiled for your information a list of your engagements. He will escort you to the dressmakers first, then to your new home. I hope you will find everything to your taste."

"But what of Peter? I can't leave without him!"

"Certainly not. I will remain with my sister. She is far too young to be sent out to find her way in the streets of Paris alone," Peter protested at the same time.

"Not alone." Talleyrand rang a small bell that rested on an oval mahogany table at his elbow. The door behind the Pendynes opened silently and a small, elderly man entered. "Ah, here is Monsieur Maigret. He will be escorting your sister and offering her every assistance. You can trust him with the young lady, I assure you, Monsieur Pendyne. He is most respectable." There was a wicked gleam in the eye of the minister, one that made it clear that he himself was certainly not respectable, that Pendyne had been right to suspect his motives, and that the Englishman would be wise to watch his sister most carefully in the future. Peter, in his distraught state, accepted it without question.

Protests seemed useless in the face of such a courteous command, and Cecie rose and made ready to leave. Again, Talleyrand lingered over her hand, and this time she did not snatch it away. But when she turned to Peter, she rose on her toes and placed a kiss on his cheek. "Do be careful," she whispered into his ear, using English.

"I shall be. And you, too, must watch your step."

Glancing at the small man who was to be her escort, she said drily, "Oh, I can take care of myself. Or rather, they shall take care of me. These poor French have never before seen such a helpless, silly female as I am about to be! They will take me for an utter fool."

"Good girl. That's a clever idea." Peter watched her leave with a better heart, then turned with a sigh to the man in the throne-like chair.

Immediately after the interview with Pendyne, the Count sat down and wrote a report on what he had learned for his Imperial master. When his thoughts wandered to Cecie, a rueful smile flitted across his face. A charming young girl, one that he was sure the Emperor would find attractive. Very attractive. He rather thought that her relationship with the Englishman was as it had been represented by them, the family resemblance and the easy familiarity of the conduct toward one another indicated such a connection. No man would treat his mistress with that touch of indifference and protectiveness.

As a diplomat and manipulator of men, it was all to the good that he should have such a valuable insurance of Pendyne's co-operation, but he feared that the young man would throw it all over for the girl's sake, if he thought she was threatened. It would be a pity to lose the services of such an able man. And he knew his Emperor well.

The next few days should be most amusing.

Twelve

It was late that afternoon before Peter saw Cecie again, standing in the drawing room of their mansion, scowling at a lady playing a piano. This was not to say that they had company already; on the contrary, the lady in question was of bronze, as was her piano, and she was playing a long florid tune as she sat in front of an elaborately contrived clock. The case of the clock showed a tiny drawing room with mirrors and windows draped in gilt. As he stared at it, the musical apparatus wound down and the playing came to an end.

"Isn't it ghastly?" Cecie asked. "She can even look at herself in these mirrors, as if all this scroll and gilt weren't enough to please her vanity. I think her music is horrid."

"Then don't wind it up."

"I shan't, now that you are here to talk to."

Peter looked at her closely. "You have a new gown."

"Yes. LeRoy, the dressmaker who makes all of the Empress's outfits, whipped it up for me. Aren't you impressed?" She spread her skirts for inspection, looking down at the blue silk of the gown all covered with bees. The bodice had been cut straight across and rather low and she was unsure that she approved entirely of the effect, although she had to allow to herself that it was the height of fashion. The skirt fell from beneath her arms in straight lines to the floor, in the classical mode, but she was more accustomed to this for the same style was popular in England. "What are these bees for? I recall seeing the same design on Talleyrand's curtains."

Peter began to laugh despite himself. " 'B.' For Bonaparte. It is one of the official Imperial emblems. They say that all the rooms of the Tuileries are draped with them."

"Surely not! I shall look just like the curtains!" she protested.

He looked at her more closely. "No, not that, Cuz. You are too pretty for anyone to mistake you for window dressing. They have cropped your hair, too."

She answered by reaching up and giving a lock a tug. "You should see the rest of this place, Peter. It is just as bad as this clock. There are no fewer than five reception rooms. Do you suppose they will expect us to entertain? I should be terrified."

"If they want us to do that, they will have to arrange it all themselves. I have had enough of the French."

114

She thought it rather late in the day to decide that, but said nothing. He looked so woebegone that she hadn't the heart to tease him with his mistakes.

"My bedroom has the oddest bed in it. It seems to be a combination Egyptian couch and tent. The canopy netting reaches all the way from an outrageously high backboard to the foot, and I will be quite enveloped by it, I assure you. It is like its own little room, almost."

"You won't have to worry about mosquitoes."

"I suppose not," she agreed giggling. "But then there is this marvelous mirror, more than six feet tall, all surrounded with winged figures who hold a medallion with an 'N' in it this time, does that mean Napoleon?, up at the top, and with garlands and butterflies interspersed, and even candelabra on either side to light it all."

"It is called a Psyche, I collect."

"How do you know?"

"The butterflies are her symbol. There is some play in which she keeps looking at her reflection in mirrors and streams of clear water. Hence the use of her name denotes these mirrors."

Cecie looked impressed. "There are a lot of cupids about, too. It is quite a love bower."

The expression on Peter's face was rigid. "It had better not become one, Cuz. Not while we are here. Do you have the key to the door? I want you to keep it locked at all times when you are in that room."

"Whatever are you so upset about?" she asked him, laughing at his ludicrous frown. He looked

115

at her sharply, seeking cynicism in her words, then with a sigh he tried to explain as tactfully as he could.

"We are very much prisoners of the French government, Cecie, for all the luxury of this cage. Talleyrand isn't sure that he trusts me, and I am being held until he can verify the information I have given him."

"Peter, whyever did you do it? Why did you break your word to me?" Her tone was no longer light and bantering and she sat down on the nearest chair, hands clasped tightly in her lap.

"I have not precisely broken my promise, Cecie. You have forgotten the exact nature of it. You must trust me."

"It is no longer a question of trust, Peter, but rather one of necessity. If you are in danger, I will do all I can to help you, while we are in France. But I would rather be thrown into a French dungeon than have you play traitor to England's safety."

"Then I will rely on you. You needn't worry, I can take care of myself once we are returned to Cornwall." She did not appear to believe him, but she let his assurance pass unchallenged.

He tried to inject a happier note into the conversation. "And what of your other dresses? Are they magnificent?"

"They are all going to be just like that material you gave me! But most aren't yet done. They have finished only this one and another day dress, which I am to wear tomorrow to a luncheon at the Tuileries."

"The Tuileries?"

She nodded her head vigorously. "Yes, exactly. The Empress herself is to be my hostess. Can you imagine?" She was a little girl again, playing at being grown up, but awed by it all.

"Good grief," Peter answered weakly. "They are doing this all with a vengeance. I had no idea we were to be treated so."

"The information you supplied to them must be very valuable, Peter."

He ignored the reproach in her voice. "It would seem so. Or they have hopes of more in the future."

Her mind turned to happier thoughts. "And they are making me the most magnificent court gown you can imagine. It even has a train, and it is embroidered all over with tiny pearls, and. . . ."

He was laughing at her by then. "Stop, stop, Cecie. All that is gibberish to me. I can't tell one lady's dress from another, except by the color."

Cecie's eyelashes lowered over her blue eyes and her expression changed to a demure one. "You managed to choose those yards and yards of fine fabric that are back home now."

"Yes, but I chose them for their colors."

For a moment she dimpled at him, then she looked at the oppressive glory about them. "What are we to do, Peter? I shall start playing horrid little tunes on the piano if we spend much time here. I shall be driven to it!" There was a note of hysteria in her voice as she spoke these last words.

He looked at her with dismay. Her earlier insouciance had convinced him that she was bearing up well under the strain of the danger they faced, and he had been half way to thinking that she failed to appreciate just how bad it all was. He realized now that if this last had been true, she might have continued in her anger toward him. Only fear was causing her to forget so easily her distaste for the crimes he had committed, and family loyalty demanded that she help him in this crisis.

"We must lull their suspicions first, Cecie. Right now we are so surrounded by spies that our every move is watched. We can not even be sure that those around us don't understand English, no matter what they claim. Every word will be recorded, unless we are careful." As he spoke these words, he had lowered his voice and leaned over her chair, until he was whispering in her ear.

"Do you mean that someone is listening now?"

"Perhaps. I think that a stroll in the garden will be in order." He walked over to the floor-length windows that opened on to the small garden in the back of the mansion and gestured for her to precede him. When they were in the safety of the garden he continued their talk.

"I don't think that you are in any danger, Cecie, unless they decide to use you against me."

"But will we ever get home? I am not sure that I believe Count Talleyrand."

"Good girl. I don't believe him, either. But I

am not without resources of my own. I studied in France for several years, as you know, and still have friends here. I will be able to get you out of the country somehow."

"But what of your own safety? Will they hold you prisoner?" she asked with despair. "I don't want to lose you, even if you have done dreadful things."

He grinned down at her. "You will have a hard time doing that. I have no intention of losing *you!*" He was pleased to see her blush when she heard this.

"First we must contrive to escape," she said briskly to hide her embarrassment.

"Quite right. And this plan to introduce us into Society may prove the kindest thing they could have done for us."

"How so? Won't it destroy your reputation? The English government is sure to hear of it and judge you by it."

"It may do that. But this ball will also give us the chance to meet people openly, and perhaps learn something of value. I will be able to get in touch with one or two friends without seeming to place great importance on it. An old school-friend is married to an intimate of the Princess Hortense, Napoleon's stepdaughter, and there are others such as my classmate in the Court. I can hope to see them at this ball. No one will be the wiser that we have known one another for many years, not if we are discreet."

"And what can I do to help?"

"You must keep your ears open. Your idea of
119

appearing foolish and silly was a good one. People may say things to you that they would ordinarily not reveal. And wives' gossip could be most helpful. Anything could help, even the information that a certain officer will be going to such and such a post. With my knowledge of what I have already told them, I may be able to judge whether they are acting on it."

"And if we get back to England soon enough, perhaps the knowledge of what the French know will help our armies and navy?" she whispered.

Peter smiled down into her anxious face. "It will do more than that, Cecie. Believe me, England will not be allowed to suffer from what I have told the French."

Touched by his renewed patriotism, and certain that it owed something to her persuasion, she smiled back at him. "Then I will do all that I can. I only wish it were more."

"It is enough."

Thirteen

The next day, as promised, a very grand carriage with the Imperial coat of arms on the door paneling arrived at the appointed hour to carry Cecie to the Tuileries. It took all her courage to enter it, and for a moment she was even afraid that her excellent French would desert her and she would be left to stutter in English. But the drive through the warm autumn air soothed her and she was even beginning to enjoy the bright, tree-lined boulevards stretching out like tunnels before her, when the carriage took a turn and she was facing the grandeur of the old Bourbon royal palace, now occupied by the Imperial Bonapartes.

They passed through the iron gate of the Carrousel into a fine open space. The courtyard where she stepped down from the carriage presented a strange appearance, being strewn with small depressions in the grass. She was later to discover that these were all that remained of the famous Trees of Liberty that had been planted during the early days of the Revolution, only to be torn up whole on the order of the First Consul Bonaparte when he moved into his official residence in the palace. Someone had failed to properly fill in the earth.

An equerry met her at her carriage door, and led her up a flight of steps to a drawing room done in violet blue fabric with some sort of light brown design embroidered all over it. It looked handsome enough by itself, but with its very modern style it did not go well with the ceilings and panelings from an older era. Cecie craned her neck to see as much as she could, staring at the molded ceiling and wishing that the windows were low enough for her to look out onto the gardens. She was even standing on tiptoe, having ignored her guide, in an effort to see through them, when a voice from behind her interrupted her.

"It is a pity, isn't it, that they placed the windows so high? It leaves the lovely view unseen."

Cecie spun around to face a tall, slender woman who was smiling at her with closed lips. For a moment, she was at a loss for words, not knowing how she was to address this unknown lady, whom she took for another guest. "Yes, it is a pity. I am used to looking out over the grounds at home, not feeling shut in in this way," she answered in her best French.

The lady's smile was even more charming.

"Ah, you must be Mlle. Pendyne, of whom Count Talleyrand has told me so much. I would wish that the windows were lower for your sake, if not mine, so that you would feel less your distance from home."

Cecie curtsied prettily and smiled back at the lady, pleased that at least one member of the luncheon party was so sympathetic. "It must be a disappointment to live without a view of trees and grass."

The lady shrugged. "One can see it from the Emperor's apartments. Perhaps in a year or two I shall ask him to alter the windows. We shall see."

With a shock Cecie noticed the small diamond tiara glittering in the woman's light brown curls and realized that she was speaking to her hostess. "Yes, Your Majesty," she murmured, awed despite herself, and she made another curtsy.

The equerry had noticed her delinquency and hurried back with bows and apologies, and a formal introduction was made, but somehow there prevailed the friendly spirit of the first few sentences they had exchanged, and the young girl found herself led into the next salon by the Empress Josephine herself.

In her excitement she didn't know where to look first. This room was done all over in yellow and brown satin, and there were mahogany chairs covered with striped satin of the same shade of yellow. The mirrors were draped in the same fabric rather than framed, adding immensely to the brightness of the room. All around

123

her rays of light seemed to dance, pouring in through the high windows and reflecting on the mirrors and jewels of the ladies present.

"I am so pleased that I arrived in Paris in time to greet you myself," the Empress told her in a confiding tone as the other ladies in the room rose to acknowledge her presence with deep curtsies. "I have only just returned from taking the waters at Plombières once again. My health is indifferent, as perhaps you are aware." She ended this with a great sigh.

Cecie was all sympathy in an instant. "It is a great pity that you cannot enjoy the benefits of a vigorous constitution. Ill health is so tiresome," she said.

"Yes. And there are so many demands that my new position make on me, receptions and audiences and of course the need to present the Emperor with an heir." Her young guest was still naive enough to blush at this casual, indiscreet mention of babies, a fact the Empress noticed with a laugh. "You will hear worse than that while visiting our Court! But how refreshing to see a girl who is still innocent and able to show it. I will keep a special eye on you, Mlle. Anglaise. This luncheon will give you an opportunity to meet some ladies and become acquainted with Court etiquette before you are presented to the Emperor. I think I will put you next to Mrs. Livingston. Although she is an American, her husband is chargé d' affaires here for that country, she will none the less speak English with you, if you need an interpreter or just feel homesick for your own language. Here is the lady now." One of the liveried equerries had already fetched the lady in question and brought her to the Empress, and the introduction was duly made. Cecie was aware that every lady in the room was straining to hear what was said, and assumed that the Empress's presence was the cause for the interest. But when her hostess had moved on to other guests, attention was still riveted on the English girl and her conversation with the American lady.

"If we speak in English no one will ever forgive us," Mrs. Livingston said gaily, in English. "Everyone is dying to know all about you, you know, and your brother, too, of course. There are all sorts of romantic tales flying about the capital about secret military information and sea battles in the Channel and spies."

She said this without malice, in the tone of one friend to another, and Cecie, despite her annoyance at the word spy, found herself grateful for the warning. The American, a petite lady with frizzed hair that fell down over her large brown eyes, had given her due warning, in their own language, of what to expect. Cecie smiled her appreciation.

"Perhaps we had best carry on our conversation in French, or they will be sure that *we* are the spies!" she suggested with a rueful laugh.

Mrs. Livingston nodded her head, her curls bobbing with vigor. "Very good, Mlle. Pendyne," she said in French. "I would be pleased to assist you in finding your way around the shops of

Paris. You must certainly buy all you can while you are here," she added, for all the world as if Cecie were a mere tourist who would be returning to England on the next Channel packet. "The dressmakers are a must for you. They are the finest in the world. We shall have such fun with your wardrobe." And with a graceful turn of her head she included another lady, a Mme. de Moncy who had been hovering quite close, in the conversation, seeking her advice on which of the modistes would be the first on the young lady's list of places to visit. The afternoon passed pleasantly with charming advice, probing curiosity, and soft spoken scandal.

When next she saw her "brother" she did not know where to begin her report. He had said he wanted to hear about all the ladies' talk, but she blushed at what she would have to say. Much of it had been barely comprehensible to her.

"There was much chatter of a Carlotta Gazzani, an Italian lady who is a reader to the Empress but who does not speak a word of French! Some of the ladies said she could not even read. The Emperor gave her the position on his last trip to Italy. How can she read if she doesn't know how to? And it was most peculiar, but they said nothing of her when the Empress was near enough to hear, but a great deal when that lady was at the other end of the room."

"I would think that the Empress speaks Italian as well as French," Peter said quickly, ignoring the latter part of the question. Whenever he got Cecie back to England, she was going to have a surprising amount of interesting gossip about the Emperor's private life; he hoped with little understanding of it.

"And the Empress took the waters at Plombières, but that is no secret, I suppose, for she was telling us of the triumphal arch they had made for her at Nancy and how she had had to make some sort of speech to thank them for it. No one seems to think that it did her any good. And there is an engagement between the daughter of the Elector of Bavaria and Eugène, the Empress's son by her first marriage. They are going to make the Princess Augusta break off another engagement for this one. And they spoke of the army poised along the coast, only they stopped talking about that when they thought that I might hear them."

Peter, who had been playing with the drooping Michaelmas daisies that bordered the garden path, was attentive once more. "That is very important, Cecie. Did they talk of any shifting of the army corps? The British navy is pretty well aware of where everything has been placed during the summer, but any news of change could be important."

She thought a moment. "Well, Mme. Murat and the marshal arrived from Boulogne but a week ago. He is supposed to be the Grand Admiral. Is that important? They can't very well launch an invasion across the Channel without their Grand Admiral present, can they?"

Casting his mind back over some of the French campaigns of the last few years, Peter shook his head. "I can't even begin to guess. Napoleon does things as he chooses, whatever is necessary to gain success. They need the help of the Spanish fleet for their undertaking. Did you hear anything of that?"

"No. They aren't very interested in anything that isn't French." She neglected to mention that she was an exception, guessing quite rightly that this would worry Peter. "There was one lady who was enormously interested in you, though."

"Oh?"

"Yes, a Mme. de Moncy. She said that she had met you when you were studying in Paris, and she was most friendly. Is that true? Do you know her?"

The color on Peter's face heightened slightly, then was gone in a flash. "Yes, I do seem to recall a lady of that name. She had only just married a man some years older than herself, but one possessed of considerable wealth."

"You seem to recall quite a bit about her!" Cecie said, a hint of concern in her voice. "I am not sure that I liked her at all well, but she insisted that she would accompany me on a drive tomorrow. I think she just wants to meet you."

"Then I will be there!" Peter said, disappointing his cousin. "She may be of the greatest help to us, you know. Her husband is an important officer under Murat's command and would know much useful information."

128

"But why should she tell us anything?"

This time the blush was even more pronounced, and lingered longer. "Perhaps for the sake of old friendship," he murmured, turning away from his cousin's clear, penetrating eyes.

"How very friendly!" she snapped before she stalked back into the house, leaving Peter to his daisies.

Fourteen

Even to Cecie's untutored eye, it was apparent that Mme. de Moncy was setting up a flirtation with her cousin Peter. The lady arrived dressed in an extreme fashion that made the most of her fine, full bosom and flawless shoulders, too much so in Cecie's opinion, for the former was near to spilling out of her bodice every time the carriage hit a rough spot in the road. No, the low line of the lady's dress, the rakish angle of the bonnet she wore, the care with which she had applied her makeup, far more of the latter than had been seen in the Empress's salon, all proclaimed loudly that Mme. de Moncy was very interested in Peter Pendyne. It was vulgar and unbecoming in the extreme.

Unfortunately, Peter seemed to reciprocate the interest.

The French lady had arrived promptly at eleven on the morning after the luncheon, all kind concern and womanly helpfulness. The little Anglaise must see something of Paris, it was an experience she would never forget!, and the shops, the very best shops, must be pointed out to her and perhaps visited briefly for a purchase or two. And Monsieur Pendyne, did he not want to renew his acquaintanceship with Paris? Many changes had come about in the years since he had last visited the French capital. He really must relearn his way around the city. His old friend from his student days, and here there was a significant pause and her voice dropped to a husky whisper, would be more than glad to act as his guide. And of course the young lady was to come, too. Would he care to join her?

He would.

And so the three of them were seated in the de Moncy carriage, trotting along the Rue Saint-Honoré, the Avenue des Champs-Elysées and the Boulevard Saint-Germaine. They saw the Cathedral de Notre Dame, the Ile Saint-Louis, admired the military precision of the Champ-de-Mars as contrasted with the student disorder of the Quartier Latin, stopping at last at the Jardin du Luxembourg to alight and enjoy the last of the summer flowers. Mme. de Moncy had spent far more of her attention on helping Peter rediscover the city than she had with Cecie's first introduction to it. Cecie felt neglected.

"And how long will you be staying in Paris, Monsieur Pierre?" Mme. de Moncy asked for the tenth time, or was it the twelfth?

"I am unable to say, madam. It rests in the hands of Monsieur Talleyrand and the Emperor."

"Then I hope that they will diddle and daddle and spend their time on other affairs. I hope that they will forget all about you, and leave you to me to take care of."

Cecie was beginning to hate the caressing tone the woman used whenever she spoke to Peter. And the Frenchified "Pierre" was nearly more than she could stomach. But her good breeding prevailed and she pouted only a little, so little that it went unnoticed by the Frenchwoman, although her cousin did regard her with a wary eye.

"Your offer is very flattering, Mme. de Moncy, especially as it comes from the wife of such an important officer. I understand that your husband is a general on Prince Murat's staff?"

"Yes, but why do you talk of him? He is far away in Boulogne, poised to invade your lovely English countryside, which is so sad, I much prefer to be at peace with Englishmen. In fact, I want very much to be friends with Englishmen!"

"But he will be on the Channel coast for some time?" Peter pressed, an insinuating note creeping into his voice. Cecie considered stalking off down a path to the left, leaving these two to their disgusting flirtation, but curiosity and perverse stubbornness stayed her.

Mme. de Moncy was suddenly more than interested in discussing her husband's whereabouts. "He will be away from Paris for many months, Monsieur Pierre, of that I assure you."

"How unfortunate for you his wife, madam," Peter murmured confidentially in her ear.

133

"Oh, just look at the lovely flower beds along this way," Cecie said in a loud determined voice.

Mme. de Moncy turned to answer her with a smiling condescension. "You must run along and admire them more closely, dear. Your interest in all things green is perhaps an English passion? The Empress found you so enormously amusing yesterday when she discovered you trying to climb on a chair to see out the windows!"

Cecie flushed furiously. "I was hardly climbing, Mme. de Moncy. And the Empress herself seemed much in sympathy with my interest. After all, she has spent a great deal of time on the gardens of her country place, Malmaison, has she not? I understand that vast sums have gone into the rose garden alone!"

Peter tried to cover Cecie's sudden change of role. "And whenever and wherever she travels she is always anxious to purchase new plants to introduce into France, is that not so?" There was no indication that he had heard the anger in Cecie's voice.

Seeing that the interest lay with Peter as much as Cecie, Mme. de Moncy agreed with her most charming smile. "Her Majesty is of great assistance to the Emperor in this. She *has* done much to encourage the introduction of new crops and plants into France."

"Most laudable!" Peter answered, ignoring Cecie all together. "Every country should be willing to try the new and unfamiliar. The introduction of new ideas and products is like an infusion of fresh blood for the nation."

"You are very sympathetic to the French nation, very sympathetic for an Englishman," madame answered in another whisper. "I find that most strange and attractive."

Their conversation continued in the lowest tones, and Cecie could barely hear her cousin's reply. "It is a sympathy founded on the appreciation of the beauty of the country."

"France is said to be the most beautiful in the world," she agreed with complaisance.

"And it has the most beautiful women to grace it, madam." He had taken her hand and was bestowing a kiss on the palm. Cecie strove to divert her attention to the dry, dying flowers around her, but she was not succeeding very well. The conversation was still just audible and despite her disgust, she was straining to hear every word of it.

"Then it is perhaps your love of beautiful women that makes you so interested in the welfare of France, Monsieur Pierre?"

"Yes, of beautiful women. And of certain ones in particular."

"Ones?"

"Shall we say just one?"

And with this, Cecie took herself off, marching toward a distant fountain. She carried herself with her greatest poise and grace, moving along the paths with the step of a young lady of quality, but her performance went unappreciated. Monsieur Pierre and Mme. de Moncy had eyes only for one another.

*   *   *

Cecie cried for a long time that night. Nothing seemed to be going as it should and she strongly suspected that her cousin was working with less than total energy on the matter of returning the two of them to England. In fact, he seemed to be content to idle away the hours cultivating the friendship of a certain French matron who was without the company of her husband at the moment. Considering what had happened that day, Cecie determined to discuss the matter with her cousin, in a mature, sensible way, as soon as possible. It was only right that she discover his plans, for they involved her so intimately. She was relying on him to arrange for her passage out of France, a task he had promised to see through to a successful conclusion. She would make him keep his word!

Then the recollection of how poorly he had done this in the past swept over her, and she wept angrily, turning her face into her damp pillow for the rest of the night.

Fifteen

That night Cecie enjoyed the comforts of her exotic bed even less than the night before. She tossed and turned in her sheets, the drapery of the tent disconcerting her on those rare occasions when she began to drift into sleep, its waving and glimmering being wholly unfamiliar to her. The root of her dismay was her inability to judge the truth of her cousin's promises. He had sounded as sweet and as reassuring to her in the garden as he ever had in the long years of their friendship, promising to help her as he ought. But back in the cave with the Holy Well, he had promised to reform and look where that had led them! If he had only given up the vainglories of this smuggling enterprise, if he had applied to her father for any monies he was in need of, if he had sought adventure honorably, in service to the Crown, as did Major Armstrong, none of this would have happened. It was all the fault of his perverse unwillingness to keep his word that she was in her present predicament. Her safety was in the gravest jeopardy and she was all but the prisoner of the French government here in Paris, nearly their slave, to do as they directed, in the hope that they would lose interest in her or decide that it was to their advantage to return her to England. All this, for want of an honorable regard for one's promise!

She decided that she must find out what she could. A chance word overheard as she mounted the stairs to her room earlier in the evening had informed her that her cousin planned to ride out very early the following morning. He had ordered his horse out for such and such an hour. Apparently his freedom of action was not to be challenged by the French, she thought angrily. Then the notion that the French had perhaps set spies on him and only wished him to rush to his downfall assailed her and she felt remorse that she had distrusted him. More confusion! In any case, she must discover more.

When dawn could be seen through her curtains, she crept out of her bed and dressed hurriedly in the same shabby old riding habit she had donned for her evening escapade in Cornwall, the least noticeable of her few garments. Thus dressed, she hoped to be able to travel the streets of Paris without attracting notice. This done, she slipped from the room, locking the door behind her, and then hurried down the stairs. As she had expected, no one was about, and she made her way unremarked to the back of the mansion.

In the stables her luck held. If she was to succeed in following Peter that day, she must have a mount of her own. And there, waiting patiently in a stall beside a larger horse, she found a brown mare with a blaze on her forehead. With quick, practical movements, she saddled the little mare and bridled her, then led her out into the street, the animal's muzzle muffled with her scarf. They made no noise as they passed through the dirt-packed yard, and soon Cecie had moved herself and her mount to a convenient vantage point in some trees a few yards down the road, just in sight of the house. There, she waited.

She had timed her egress from the mansion well, for in less than fifteen minutes her cousin left the yard, mounted on the black stallion that had neighbored her mare. Moving cautiously, her usually forgotten veil pulled over her face, Cecie set out to follow. The two riders, one moving briskly and confidently, the other holding back shyly, moved toward the outskirts of Paris and were soon far from the normal travelers and pedestrians of the city's streets. They passed along country paths until the leader pulled into a little wood and stopped.

This time it was a longer wait. Cecie smothered her impatience by enjoying the beauty of their little copse. She was standing with her mount just out of sight of Peter's position in an open field, hidden by a curve of the land. The field where her quarry lingered was filled with the remains of its summer glory, and soon Peter was picking a bouquet as if to fill the time. Comfortable in her shade, Cecie listened to the birds singing, smelled the woodsy air, and sat on a grassy patch under a tree while she watched.

More than an hour after their arrival, the sound of other hooves were heard approaching, and Cecie moved to her horse's head to assure the mare's silence. She was just able to see the newcomer, another lady dressed in a fine velvet habit of salmon pink decorated with lace at the throat, wrist and petticoat, when her view was obscured by the very rise of ground that hid her. She could not see what took place with any ease, for that would mean the risk of leaving her horse, but she soon discovered that she was well situated to hear all that was said in the field.

"Pierre, my love!" the lady said in French, her words accompanied by the sound of her dismounting and the flurry of the horses.

"Marie, I thought you would never come!" Peter replied.

"It is too bad of you to expect a lady to come out at such an uncivilized hour, Pierre," she purred. "But what have you brought me?"

Peter laughed. "I did not precisely bring it, darling, rather I found it here. It is a bouquet of flowers that are not nearly lovely enough for you. Will you accept them as a peace offering for my barbaric choice of time?"

Cecie heard a low gurgle of feminine laughter, followed by a long silence. She realized now, to her horror, that she had found her cousin not

140

in any sort of treasonous business, or even in untreasonous business, but rather in the business of love. She had followed him to an assignation with Mme. de Moncy! Cecie's cheeks burned with shame as she realized that she had put herself in the most degrading of positions, that of spying on the conduct of another's love affair. Her only thought was to take herself off as quickly as she could.

It was as she was riding toward Paris, praying that she did not lose her way, that she began to consider her cousin's conduct. In the midst of dangers, political intrigue, stranded in a foreign country, he was spending time to meet a lady in secret. A married lady. How could he?

The closer she was to Paris, the greater her anger. How could he? How dare he! She was depending on him to extricate her from this coil and return her safe to her parents' home, and look how he conducted himself! In her mind, his actions were fast becoming very nearly treasonous. To set up a flirtation, nay, an affair, when surrounded on all sides by the French enemy, and to chose a Frenchwoman as his partner in this escapade were unforgivable, the worst treason he could commit. He had not only betrayed his country, he had betrayed his own family and her trust and dependence in him. He was past redemption.

She made her way through the streets of Paris with little thought, but her mare knew or guessed the way for her. Some yards from the house, she dismounted and sent the horse on ahead to the stable with a slap on the rump. Let the stableboy sort out the mystery of who had saddled the animal and taken her out for a ride. She, Cecie, must somehow creep back into the mansion, unobserved, and return to her locked bedroom before anyone guessed her absence. She approached the house with caution.

Only the indolence of the servants enabled her to carry out her purpose. She slipped through the unattended front door, her boots thoughtfully removed outside and in her stockinged feet, and ran up the wide stairs. She was in the haven of her room, behind a stout, locked door, without being seen.

In one way at least she could count herself lucky. No one would know of her little venture into the early morning countryside surrounding Paris!

In this last she was wrong, very wrong. Although her cousin Peter remained in ignorance, others had noted her departure on the mare. In fact, the horse had been placed in the stables in the hope that just such a thing would happen. A Frenchman, a spy in the pay of Fouché, the French minister of police, saw her leave and followed her. He in turn was followed by another Frenchman, a spy in the pay of Count Talleyrand. And of course, Peter had had his two trailing spies.

So they had made a merry little cavalcade through the streets of Paris, down the country lanes of the suburbs, one after the other, and out to the rendezvous in the woods. Peter and

142

Cecie, preoccupied with their own thoughts, had not noticed the procession stringing out behind them, although Peter had expected an escort of some sort. All the spies were well aware of one another's company, and soon fell into amiable disagreement as they tried to hit upon some scheme for sharing their task and avoiding unnecessary work. There was no point in having all four of them sitting out in the hot sun. Cecie's unexpected return to the mansion had thrown all this into disarray, and two spies, willy-nilly, rode home. Napoleon's ministers got their money's worth, after all.

Sixteen

The moment when Cecie faced Peter with her anger was not a propitious one for her purposes. Her cousin had been gone all day, having left early in the morning to meet Mme. de Moncy, and he had not been seen since. This was a double insult to Cecie, that he had absented himself when she wanted to speak to him, and that he had done so for the company of the Frenchwoman for whom she felt such suspicion and contempt. When he did arrive back at their borrowed mansion, she had just finished arraying herself for the ball at the Tuileries, and was standing in the smaller of the reception rooms, admiring her finery in a mirror. Peter would have scant time to prepare himself for the evening, and the course she had chosen would allow him even fewer minutes for his appearance. Unaware of her anger, he readily answered her summons and joined her by the fire.

"I have wanted to speak to you all day, but

you were never here for me to do so," she began in a confused way, using their own tongue.

"I have been out on business," he answered with good humor, missing her mood. He looked very handsome as he stood by the flickering flames, his color high and a satisfied look on his face. She stared at the disheveled appearance of his neck-cloth and felt her lip curl with disdain, but she was determined to hold to her purpose and ignore this provocation. Her resolve returned and brought her poise with it.

"Then you have arranged for my passage to England?"

He glanced up at her as he noticed the cool tone she used. "Not quite, Cuz, but things are set in motion. You sound as if you have changed your mind about it. Have you succumbed to the glories of Imperial France?" he teased.

She swept a disdainful look down his figure. "Hardly. I am as loyal to my homeland as ever. It would seem that this isn't true of both of us."

"What do you mean by that?"

"You seem to be taking an unconscionably long time in planning our escape. That is what I mean. And your planning consists of mostly dalliance with a married woman, a French lady whose husband is an officer in the Imperial army. I find your behavior all too easy to interpret, to my grief."

"You don't know what you speak of," he answered, his impatience rising.

"I know too well!" She was aware that on this night she looked her best. Her gown was one of
146

pale blue silk, embroidered all over with flowers, the V-shape of the neck and clinging drapes of the skirt showing her unaccustomed womanliness to all who cared to notice. With an elegant and disdainful flick of her wrist, one that would have done an experienced Court lady credit, she twitched her train around and seated herself in a brocaded chair. From there she gazed up at him with chilling blue eyes. She was determined to press her point home, using every weapon, including her appearance, at her disposal.

For the first time Peter was aware of her as a worthy adversary. The grandeur of her gown accounted for it in part, but her bearing did far more. His cousin was no longer little, in fact, she was near to ruining all his plans with her suspicions. He felt compelled to take some action to prevent her from doing so, or at least neutralize her interference, but his mind refused to grip the problem and he stood there like an errant schoolboy.

"You have no intention of returning to England, do you?" she asked with cool dignity. "You intend to stay here with that woman."

As this was the farthest thing from his intentions, he relaxed and smiled at her with unaffected amusement, taking the chair opposite her. His attitude did little to soothe her anger.

"In fact, you love her. It is terribly convenient for you that her husband is away right now, but that will not last forever. Then what will you do? Hang about Paris like a love-struck farm boy?"

"No. I had rather thought of taking my love back to England with me. It is my homeland after all, and I find that I prefer the English way of doing things." His voice was gentle and caressing as he smiled at her across the uncertain light.

"The English way!" she said with awful emphasis. "The English way is not to make love to another man's wife. That is the act of a rake, a scamp of the worst sort." Her dignity had deserted her and she was spitting out the words.

Despite herself, Peter was stung by her charges. "I will take you back to England, as I promised! I've always intended to do so," he snapped.

Cecie failed to consider the full significance of his words and continued her attack. "I care not what you do, as long as I am back in my home before this affair has ruined my reputation."

"You are late in thinking of that!"

"It has been the company you have thrust on me that has made me realize my position. Mme. de Moncy in particular is an unsavory type."

"Damn it, girl, can't you behave with sense? Your jealousy of this woman could put all our plans in the gravest danger."

"I am not jealous."

"Just yesterday at the Luxembourg Gardens, you would not rest until you had rebutted her mockery, mockery that was very much to our purpose. We had agreed that the appearance of a silly, foolish girl would go far toward protecting you from suspicion and would allow you to hear
148

more than would be in the ordinary way of things. It was your own idea!"

"She was being very rude!"

"Certainly she was. And you should have ignored her, or taken advantage of it, but what must you do instead but bristle and mount a counterattack that made it all too obvious that you were no fool at all. If the woman weren't so stupid she would wonder at that."

"She was too stupid to notice anything but her own malice." These words were uttered before she realized that he had anticipated her. "A fine lover you are, insulting her like that."

"I am not her lover. You don't even know what the word means."

"I will know altogether too much about it if I remain in this country much longer, and under your feeble protection."

"If you will be quiet for a moment and listen to me, you will find that I have not forgotten your welfare. I will see you back to England."

"Are you sure that there will be room on the *Mary Ann* for all of us? I doubt that Mme. de Moncy and I would be very comfortable travel companions."

"I am not taking that woman back to England with me!" Peter found that his brief anger was abating, and he lowered his tone to a more reasonable level. "Everyone in the house can hear us. Do be more careful, Cecie. I assure you that I have every intention of rescuing you from

149

your own foolishness. All of it. And I will do so gladly."

"I don't want your help!" She leaped up and began pacing up and down the room, swishing her train in her agitation.

"Well, you will have to settle for it. I will be returning to England in any case, you might as well accompany me." His manner was now one of solemnity, a solemnity she would have suspected if she had not been so full of passion against him.

"So you will recover your Englishness?" she asked harshly.

"Yes. I am tired of clocks that play abominable music, and of ladies who want to go riding at one hour and appear at another, and of cousins who don't know what they are about."

"I will be in England, too, so that last will not be remedied."

"Then I will have to change the relationship, won't I?"

"You are impossible. I don't understand a word of any of this!"

He now wore a happy, dreamy expression. "And there is also good plain English cooking. And ale. And people who will look you in the eye and tell you their minds plainly. Frenchmen are so slippery," he ended, grinning.

"You are just like Count Talleyrand, so I can't see what you have to complain about!" When she spoke the name of that august and powerful minister, her voice lowered cautiously despite her anger. Talleyrand's power over them was enough to cause her to be afraid, and fear soon overcame anger.

"What are you to do but accept my help? And while you are at it, you might deign to offer some in return."

"I will not listen at keyholes!"

"Why not? Everyone else does. Including your friend the Empress. They say she spies on the Emperor every chance she gets!"

"I will not pay any attention to you."

"You must." Here he rose to his feet and reached her side with one long stride. Hands on her shoulders, he swung her around to face him, a thing she did without relish. Blue eyes fought blue eyes, until she felt her gaze drop despite her best efforts.

"We are in the greatest danger, a fact of which I am fully aware, even when in the company of Mme. de Moncy. Especially with her. You must stop this foolishness and conduct yourself with dignity and decorum, otherwise our position will be even worse. If you can't trust me, at least be discreet for your own sake. I will do all I can to protect you, but we are far from home." She opened her mouth as if to start a counterattack, but he forestalled her. "You would not be here except for your own actions. I didn't invite you to board my boat, Cecie. If it weren't for you, I could have ended this farce long ago and fled the country."

Confusion and contrition filled her and she

looked at him with dismay in her eyes. Then suspicion reasserted itself and she drew back from him. "I don't know what to believe any more," she murmured.

"Then believe your heart, Cecie. It is a stout English one, and Cornish as well, so you can rely on it."

"That tells me little."

"A pity. I had hoped that it would tell you everything, as much as you have told me." He smiled down, his eyes filled with tenderness. "You are really a most vexing little scamp. None of this would have happened if you had sat home like a proper young lady and heeded my promise."

The memory of their moment beside the Holy Well caused Cecie's eyes to fill with tears, and she turned away, fighting despair. This failed to daunt her cousin, whose attention was drawn to the chiming of yet another gilt clock on a table in the corner.

"Dash it all! I shall be late if I don't hurry. You should not have taken so much of my time." And ignoring her look of indignation, he hurried from the room.

Seventeen

The press of carriages delayed them as they neared the Tuileries. They had left their mansion some thirty minutes later than planned, only to discover that fashionably late in Paris was even later than fashionably late in London, so they were right on time. Cecie, nervous about what was after all her debut into High Society, albeit French High Society, took comfort in the knowledge that their carriage was as elegant as any of the others she was staring at from behind the narrow windows. She only hoped that others who were staring back would appreciate the elegant picture the Pendynes presented. Peter seemed to be paying more attention to the comforts of the seat cushions.

As they neared the head of the line of equipage, he turned to her for one last reminder. "I may need you to help me with meeting friends unnoticed. You will co-operate, won't you?"

Her temper long since past, she turned to

pout at him in the dark. "I suppose I must, but what can I do?"

"Certain people may need to be distracted at certain times, more than that I can't foresee. You will make yourself agreeable to them, contrive to hold them in conversation. That is all."

"It sounds simple enough. I suppose you don't want Talleyrand to be trailing about after you."

She caught a glimmer of his white teeth as he smiled. "I doubt that he would deign to do so in any case. He undoubtedly has his well paid spies among the guests here tonight. They will do that for him."

"Then why need I bother? It doesn't sound like it would do any good."

"I have in mind a smoke screen of sorts, and in that you will be most helpful."

"Smoke screen?"

But they had reached the gate and their carriage lumbered into the courtyard that she had seen on her earlier visit. This time they were led to a different part of the palace, to the Gallery of Diana, where first the kings of France, and now the Emperor of the French, entertained their subjects. The room itself, although large and magnificently proportioned, reflected this dichotomy of history. The ceilings were of the period of the Roi-Soleil, the walls and furniture were decorated in the style favored by the moderns. Despite this clash, Cecie caught her breath at the sight of such grandeur. The huge room was lit by a myriad of candles twinkling and reflecting in the prisms of priceless chandeliers,

154

and the whole was reflected and increased by the many mirrors hanging on the walls. Peter lead her to the master of ceremonies and gave their names without her taking any notice of where she was going and what was being said around her. Then they were among the other guests.

"Mlle. Pendyne, Monsieur Pendyne, how pleased I am that you have come!" Count Talleyrand was standing near the entrance of the grand room, to all appearances acting the part of host. The Imperial couple were nowhere to be seen. "You look charming, quite charming tonight, Mademoiselle. Is the gown from LeRoy's? I thought I detected his style in it. You are one of the most elegant ladies in the room tonight."

Unsure of how to take these compliments, and unaided by any word from Peter, who seemed to be annoyed, Cecie blushed and curtsied. "Yes, it is from LeRoy's."

"You have been well advised." The older man was smiling down at her with amusement and Cecie felt that she had been gauche.

"Mrs. Livingston was kind enough to advise me in the selection of the style and colors," she added.

"Mrs. Livingston is a lady of impeccable taste. But I am sure that the final decision was yours, Mlle. Pendyne!"

"I do not see the Emperor and the Empress present, Count Talleyrand," Peter said as the Frenchman was leaning over Cecie's hand yet again. The sudden change of topic disturbed the minister not at all and he finished his pretty flourish before answering.

"It is customary for them to enter later in the evening, after all the guests have arrived. They will then circulate among their subjects and meet some of those who have not been presented. The dancing follows. It is rather formal, at least to begin with. But Mademoiselle has already met the Empress and has made herself very popular with Her Majesty, so you will undoubtedly be favored with a word or two of conversation."

"How fortunate," Cecie said in a faint voice.

"You must allow me to point out a few of the personalities among the guests, Mlle. Pendyne. I am sure that you will find many of them amusing."

Cecie suspected that if the other guests weren't amusing, Minister Talleyrand's description of them would be, and told him so with a dimpled smile. She was just accepting his arm before starting their circuit of the gallery, when Peter interrrupted again.

"I understand that there are refreshments to be found in the adjacent rooms. Cecie, you were complaining of hunger pangs, shall we adjourn there to appease them?" And with an expression that brooked no argument, he took her firmly by her other arm and began to steer her away from Count Talleyrand. The Count was even more amused.

"But of course, Mlle. Pendyne, you must visit the supper room. The food and wine there are exquisite, I assure you. No expense has been spared."

Cecie, who had had a substantial meal before leaving the mansion, started to protest, but found that Peter's foot was nudging her ankle. With poor grace, she smiled and agreed to this change of plans, then allowed him to lead her off. A backward glance over her shoulder told her that Talleyrand was taking this rebuff with his usual good humor, although his eyes lingered on her figure as she moved into the crowds. She flashed him a brilliant smile and then turned to Peter to scold him roundly.

"I am not hungry. If you neglected to eat anything before coming, that is your own fault. You shouldn't have dragged me off like that!"

"And you should have better sense than to think of sauntering off with one of the most notorious lechers in France!"

"Lecher? Is he really? I never would have guessed, his manners are so perfect. I don't know that I have ever met one before!" She sounded pleased with the discovery, pleased and curious. "Do let's go back to him!"

"Cecie! What are you saying? And this is no pleasure outing! We have work to do."

"I thought that you had work to do. I want to talk more with Count Talleyrand. You let me know when you need me." She started to turn away from him but he kept a firm grip on her arm.

"Don't be silly."

Their argument was interrupted by a fanfare

157

of trumpets announcing the arrival of their Imperial host and hostess, and they were forced to stop where they were and wait, as etiquette demanded.

The Emperor's circuit of the room was a remarkably brisk one. In fact, one of the ladies in attendance, who had been blessed with very short legs, had to hitch up her train and dash after him to keep up. He said few words, and these mostly to the gentlemen present, although Cecie could see that Josephine was pausing frequently for a charming comment here and there. The crowd around the Pendynes suddenly disappeared, and Cecie realized that they were in fact to be granted a few gracious words, as Talleyrand had predicted. Josephine was smiling at the girl with special warmth.

"Your Majesty, may I present Mlle. Pendyne, my newest friend? And her brother, Monsieur Peter Pendyne. They have but recently come to France."

Cecie dropped her deepest curtsy, staring at the face of the man standing before her. He was much shorter than his wife, far too short to be a general and an Emperor, but such he was. Napoleon smiled down at her, then reached out to capture one of her hands and raise it to his lips.

"Lovely, quite lovely. You are yet another reason for me to conquer England, Mlle. Pendyne. I had no idea that Englishwomen were so beautiful. Once this becomes known among my soldiers, there will be no stopping them."

Cecie, who was shocked by the vivid images
158

of invasion that these few words conjured in her mind, answered without thinking. "Beauty thrives in peace and security, Sire. I doubt that you would find much of it left after England was swept by war. You would be defeating your own purpose."

At first she thought that she had spoken too rashly, for a frown began to pucker between his eyes and spread down his face. Then a twinkle of amusement flashed out and he smiled at her. "Bravely spoken, Mlle. Cecilia. May I call you Cecilia? I am told that that is your Christian name, a most charming one. You must allow me to pursue this topic with you at another time when we can be more private. Like all women, you favor peace, but the harsh realities of the world make that impossible. I will explain it all to you." And he turned and moved to another part of the crowd.

"Oh, dear!" Cecie whispered in English when she had found her voice.

" 'Oh, dear!' is right," Peter said. She could not understand the depths of anger in his voice and turned to defend herself.

"I may have spoken hastily, but as you can see, he didn't mind, Peter, so you have no right to sound so foreboding."

"It is the fact that he didn't mind that worries me, Cecie. He is altogether too friendly," he answered, but the girl found little that would convince her in this cryptic reply, and she turned her back to him angrily.

The crowd around them relaxed, for the Emperor had stopped exchanging gracious words with his subjects, and they could move about again, some to preen themselves on the attention that had been paid them, others to go off and nurse their panic, having been completely ignored. Peter resumed steering Cecie to the refreshments.

"Now, we must work quickly, Cuz. You wait right here for me. Don't move under any circumstances!" and he was gone.

Cecie stood where she had been told, fuming with frustration. He had left her in a small alcove near the food tables, but too far away for her to serve herself. There she could do nothing but sit, even the small solace of food denied her.

"Mlle. Pendyne, what a pleasant surprise to meet you here! And to find you alone is an unhoped for piece of luck!"

Cecie looked up to see Captain Duval beaming down at her. She rose and said what was courteous, then allowed him to join her on the sofa. Anything was better than sitting there indefinitely by herself. A brisk and cordial conversation ensued, laced with much bantering flirtation on the captain's part, and she found herself beginning to enjoy the evening again. The gallant officer even fetched her a plate of food, something she found she needed after the turmoil and excitement of the last few hours.

The captain was just beginning to whisper audacious words of love in her ear, and she was framing amiable and noncommital replies in her mind, when Peter returned. "Cecie, come along.

160

There is someone you must meet," he said gruffly. Once again, he wore an angry expression on his face. To the captain's dismay, he carried her off to the other end of the gallery, where a series of smaller, more private alcoves were hidden from view behind velvet drapery.

"You must go into the one at the far end, taking the corridor along there to reach it. Don't let anyone see you," he whispered in her ear.

"What is this all about?" she grumbled. "Just as I was having a good time, you interfered. You always interfere."

"It is important that the person in that room stay there, do you understand? Everyone must think that I am . . . , well, just go in and talk for all you are worth. And wait for me."

"Oh, all right."

Cecie reached the door of the alcove without being seen in a matter of a few minutes. It is impossible to imagine her shock when she opened it and saw who was waiting there. Sitting on a tiny, fragile sofa, resplendent in crimson satin and ostrich feathers and lace, her face carefully powdered and her hair swept up into an alluring pile of curls, was Mme. de Moncy. For a moment, Cecie was at a loss for words.

"What are you doing here!" the lady exclaimed, with her show of irritation marring the perfection of her mouth.

"I am just looking for my brother, Mme. de Moncy. Have you seen him about?" Cecie asked with her most inane smile.

"Your brother? He left me here not five minutes ago and I don't know what has become of him. There may be very little time left for us!" She looked at Cecie sharply. "For heaven's sake, whatever you are doing, don't push your way into any more of the alcoves, people meet there for privacy." Too late, Mme. de Moncy realized that she had said the wrong thing, for Cecie entered her own alcove and sat down on a slender chair near the drapes. She looked immovable.

"Then I must stay with you! I wonder where in the world he could be? I could have sworn that I saw him enter this little room and not come out. It is most private, you are right, but why in the world do people need privacy when they could be enjoying the pleasures of such a wonderful ball?" Her eyes wide and innocent, Cecie didn't wait for the poor lady to answer, although she was pleased to see that her naive questions had flustered the Frenchwoman's calm. Somehow she continued her prattle, ignoring protests and pleas that she leave that Mme. de Moncy was occasionally able to interject into the flow of her chatter.

After some twenty minutes, Cecie was nearly at her wit's end for subjects to talk about. She was considering embarking on the whole of it again, when a gentle tap on the door warned the ladies that someone was joining them. To Cecie's immense relief, it was Peter.

"Peter, there you are! I have been looking all over for you! I was afraid that I had lost you."

"Cecie, what are you doing here?" he said with brotherly irritation. It was most awkward to have one's sister (even if she isn't one's sister) present at one's assignation with a married lady (even if one had invited the sister to come), or at least it ought to be, and he was suitably annoyed. Cecie, her high spirits returning, giggled at him.

"I had just a question or two to ask you."

He sighed.

"Perhaps we can talk outside. It will only take a moment, if Mme. de Moncy will excuse us."

Once in the corridor, she began shaking with laughter. "You should have seen the look on her face!" she crowed.

Peter grinned at her. "I can imagine. You have done your job well. Now run along and enjoy the dancing. I will be with you in a few minutes."

Cecie, stung by the realization that he intended to rejoin the lady after all, stopped laughing. "A few minutes, or a few hours?" she asked tartly.

He was still grinning at her when he answered. "A few minutes only. Wait back at that other alcove. Maybe your poor Captain Duval will still be hanging about and will entertain you."

"*Poor* Captain Duval? How dare you belittle one of my flirts? I like him far better than *your* Mme. De Moncy."

"So do I. Now, scoot." And he was back in the private room before she could protest further.

In her indignant frame of mind, Cecie took a wrong turn on the way back to the Gallery of Diana. She did not discover this until she was in a part of the palace wholly unfamiliar to her, and one that was only dimly lit. She tried to retrace her steps as best she could, but became even more confused about her direction. A door behind her opened unexpectedly and she jumped around to face whoever it was, a little frightened by her situation.

"Excuse me, sir, but I am lost. Could you tell me how to return to the ball room?" she asked in a breathless voice.

The man, a short one dressed in the most expensive and ornate of uniforms, stepped into the flickering light of a wall sconce and smiled at her. To her shock, she saw that she had accosted the Emperor Napoleon.

"Mlle. Cecie, the very person I was thinking of. What a charming coincidence!" He leaned over her hand while she executed an awkward curtsy. "How did you come to be here? Did Constant bring you?"

"Constant?"

"My valet. He frequently acts as a go-between and guide for my special friends. My very special friends." He still held her hand and she was unsure of whether she ought to retrieve it or curtsy again, then realized that he had asked her a question.

"I got lost. It was silly of me, but I wasn't paying proper attention. I was looking for my brother, you see."

"Your brother?" Judging from his expression, she knew that he didn't believe a word of her tale, but she also saw that that mattered not at all. "Your brother is a fortunate man. But I am

164

now claiming your company, and your brother, and all the other gentlemen who admire you, will have to wait."

"My company?"

"Yes, we have much to talk about. Do you not recall our conversation out there in the ball room?" He had drawn her hand through the crook of his arm and was patting it while it rested there.

"I can't imagine that you would want to talk to me!" she said nervously. "Could we do so in the ball room?"

He chuckled delightedly. "No, not at all. It is far too crowded there. You must join me in my study, where we will be most private. No one will interrupt us there." Still patting her captive hand, he turned back to the door he had just closed, and Cecie was forced to follow.

Eighteen

The study to which the Emperor led her was remarkably different from her father's at Penrith Hall. In fact, she wondered if it was used for such a purpose, the furnishings being more fitting for a boudoir than a man's workroom. Two soft armchairs graced the fireplace, an elegant sofa stood to one side in the corner, and on a table on the other side of the room were decanters of wine and glasses. A large, detailed map had been carelessly tossed onto the floor near the table, where it lay partially unrolled to reveal a glimpse of Austria's borders. Corsican green and the inevitable bees were everywhere. Aside from the map, it had the appearance of a place for social niceties, not ink-stained labor.

"What do you think of my study, Mademoiselle?" the Emperor asked, a smile playing on the corners of his mouth and eyes as he looked over her elegant figure.

"It is most attractive, Sire. Most comfortably

furnished." To her annoyance, Cecie found herself curtsying to the man once again. Something of the grandeur of the surroundings and the obsequious demeanor of all those around him had forced itself upon her sensibilities, overriding her English common sense.

"You have succeeded most admirably in your plans, Mlle. Cecilia," he said in a soft tone.

"Plans?" She was caught off guard by his unexpected comment, so that her answer was more frank than it might have been. "My plans have been to return to my homeland, Sire, and I have not been successful in achieving that. Far from it; it seems farther away than ever."

"But you have also taken a hand at spying, is this not so? And what could be a greater achievement for a spy than to visit my most private study?" He was waving a sheaf of papers that had lain on the table near the wine, wagging them almost playfully at her.

Cecie felt her breath knocked out of her by the shock of this accusation. "Whatever can you mean?" she managed to whisper.

"Just yesterday, you followed someone in the early morning hours to a most secret rendezvous in the countryside."

She felt her knees give way beneath her and sank into the nearest chair. Etiquette could go hang. "How did you know that?"

"My eyes are everywhere and see everything."

"You had me followed!"

By now he was laughing at her and she had

168

quite forgotten to be awed by him. "Not I, but rather my ministers."

"Count Talleyrand, I suppose."

"Yes, and Monsieur Fouché. It is a pity that they did not consult on their schemes beforehand. It would have been embarrassing if you or your brother had encountered any of their army of spies during the course of your ride. And money could have been saved, not that anyone thinks of that around here," he grumbled.

"I should have known!" she said cursing herself inwardly for her own stupidity.

"And so, I must ask you why you did such a thing. Are you jealous of your brother's friendship with the charming Mme. de Moncy? Sisters should learn to accept such things from the men of their family. It is the way of the world." He had filled two glasses with wine and walked across the Turkish rug before the fireplace to put one in her hand. "Or is it part of a more interesting treachery?" He stood above her, smiling down into her eyes.

Cecie took her courage in hand and decided to tell him the truth or at least part of it. "I am not precisely jealous of Mme. de Moncy, Sire."

"I am glad to hear that. Perhaps as you become more conversant with the ways of love, you will understand your brother's actions and have more sympathy for them." His eyes were playing over the detail of her dress, lingering at the bodice and shoulders.

"Yes, perhaps," she said quickly, trying to

169

ignore his expression and tone. "But you see, it worries me for very practical reasons."

"Oh?" His eyebrows were raised with surprise, but the smile still showed on his lips.

"I am afraid that he will forget to take me back to England. That he will think it too much of a bother, what with Mme. de Moncy here to pay court to. He may decide that he doesn't want to go back at all!"

"And that would dismay you? You fear that if he does not go, you will not? After several days enjoying the hospitality of France, you would still turn your back on her and embrace our greatest enemy?" His voice was angry, but the remnants of the smile in his eyes told her that she had not roused any real fury.

"But you see, it is my home," she said with beguiling simplicity. "My mama and papa and all I hold dear are in Cornwall."

She was surprised to see his expression change and soften as a look of tender sympathy stole over his face. "Ah, yes, it is right for so young a girl to long for the comfort of her parents. It is altogether fitting that you feel this way. But you must realize that some day you will leave them. You cannot cling to your childhood forever!"

She bowed her head to hide a smile of amusement as she heard this pompous lecture. "Yes, Sire."

"And perhaps now is the time for you to unfurl your wings, little one." His hand reached out to tilt her chin so that he could look at her eyes once more. "And it would be very difficult for your brother when he gets back to England, very difficult indeed. They would call him a traitor, I fear, no matter what Talleyrand says he can do to change it. He would be thrown into prison. And they would say cruel things about you, too, my child. Cruel and ugly things, which would be a pity for one so young and beautiful to suffer. So I must advise you to stay here in France and urge your brother to do the same. I will personally see that you want for nothing."

His face had moved closer and closer to her own as he spoke, until she could see nothing but his eyes peering intently into her own. Panic took hold of her and she opened her mouth to gasp for breath, a rash act in view of his intentions. His lips were just beginning to seek her own when a furious pounding on the door shattered the quiet of the room.

"Bonaparte!"

"Damn!" Napoleon jerked himself upright and stood glaring at the door, legs astride the valuable carpet, hands on hips.

"Bonaparte, I know you are in there!" a feminine voice shrieked. "Let me in at once. You are with that young English girl, I can tell. I know! I demand that you admit me at once."

"I am at work with Monsieur Castelot. Do not disturb me!"

"Monsieur Castelot is in the ballroom dancing the waltz at this very moment. You cannot trick me with such a shabby lie."

"You will return to your guests immediately!" he roared.

It was to no avail. "It is absurd for you to claim that you are working in the middle of a ball, Bonaparte. Now let me in!"

Josephine rattled the handle of the door as if she would twist it from the wood that held it, and Napoleon began to pace up and down the room with agitation, his hands clasped behind his back and his head lowered in thought.

"I saw you leave the gallery to follow her!"

All the while this marital quarrel raged, Cecie was pressing herself into her chair, wishing to be anywhere but in that study. She was amazed by what she had heard. For the Empress of the French to be scolding the Emperor her husband like a common fisherwoman, forgetting the barest courtesy and personal dignity and even the etiquette due to the man as Emperor, horrified her. Josephine was shouting at the Emperor, the Napoleon who commanded armies and had conquered Europe, as if he were plain Monsieur Bonaparte. And there she sat listening!

"We have gone through this before, Josephine," he said through the door, his tone and manner calm. "It has done you no good before, and it will be no different now. You must return to your guests."

"They are your guests too," a peevish voice answered.

"Go back to the ball!" he roared.

"Bonaparte!" the poor lady was now wailing in what sounded to Cecie to be real distress, and it was this that finally forced the girl to act. Before he could intercede, she had run across the room to the door and turned the key in the lock.

"There is nothing for you to be jealous of, Your Majesty," she said to the distraught woman who faced her. "He thinks I am a spy. He has had men following me, or rather Monsieur Talleyrand and Monsieur Fouché have done that for him, and he is now proving to his satisfaction that I am a dangerous criminal!"

Josephine stared into wide blue eyes, eyes filled with tears and fear and innocence, and capitulated to the girl and her tale. "Don't be ridiculous, Bonaparte. She is just a sweet, foolish young girl who had the misfortune to stumble into her brother's evil activities. You must not frighten her so." She took her own handkerchief and dabbed the girl's tears, slipping her arm around her heaving shoulders. "Now, now, I will see that nothing happens to you! You are quite safe, isn't she, Bonaparte?"

The accusing eyes and demanding voice would accept no argument, and the Emperor of the French retreated. "It was a joke. I had hoped that she would say something revealing about her brother," he said in a sulky voice.

"You should be ashamed of yourself! Now, Mademoiselle, you will calm yourself and return to the ballroom and the Emperor and I will discuss the fastest and safest way of returning you to your father and mother. Won't we, Bonaparte?"

"Of course, dearest."

"There, see? Now run along, Mlle. Pendyne. Leave it to me, all will be well."

Clutching the Empress's lace handkerchief to her eyes, Cecie scampered into the hall and left the Imperial couple to make their peace.

Nineteen

The first person she encountered after she escaped the Emperor's study was her cousin Peter, a happenstance whose benefit she soon had cause to question.

"Where have you been?"

"I got lost in the corridors. . . ."

"I have been searching for you nearly this whole hour past. Surely there was someone to point out the way?"

"Well, I met only one person and he. . . ."

"And you stopped to flirt with him like a shameless hussy."

"I did not!"

"You are worse than that de Moncy creature!"

"You like her company well enough for all that, and don't you dare to criticize me, Peter!"

"How could you linger with some strange man in those dark corridors? Have you no sense of decency?"

"I did not linger with some strange man. I had been introduced to him. . . ."

"My God, was it Talleyrand? He's old enough to be your father!"

"It was not the Count!"

"Then who?"

"The Emperor!"

"The Emperor?" The shocked look on Peter's face confirmed her worst fears of the position she had been in.

"Yes."

"Young girls don't just talk to Napoleon."

"He accused me of spying, Peter, and that is your own fault." Her words were less than just but she could not bare to have him get the best of her.

Her cousin's anger drained away. "Are you serious? On what did he base it?"

Cecie thought quickly. She couldn't admit that she had followed Peter the morning before and been followed in turn herself. "He said that I was poking down that corridor for that purpose," she explained at last. "Although I don't think he believed it himself. He just wanted to frighten me. He thought that someone named Constant had brought me. It was most peculiar."

Her confusion over the sordid details of her experience stopped the flurry of doubts in his mind. He searched her face, seeking an answer to the questions that plagued him, and she met his look with her eyes veiled with innocence. It was this lack of her usual guile, for he knew her as well as she knew him, that reassured him. He had long since learned that when Cecie looked her most innocent she was up to some mischief.

"Exactly what happened?"

Something in his quiet, careful tone told her that he was no longer angry and she answered truthfully. "He teased me about spying and he flirted with me a bit and I think he was going to kiss me, but then his wife came."

"His wife?"

"Yes, his wife. The Empress. And she began pounding on the door demanding to be let in."

"And was she?" He was starting to grin despite himself.

"Well, at first he told her to go away, and they shouted at each other for some minutes and then she began to cry. . . ."

"And?"

"And I let her in."

A look of dawning respect crossed Peter's face. "How diabolically clever of you, love. And it was so simple! You managed to fend off one who has not heard the word 'no' for many years, and. . . ." He had to stop, his laughter was choking him so.

"Well, I couldn't have done it without the Empress. She even promised to find me a passage home!"

"How generous of her!"

They stood leaning against the wall, grinning happily over the details of Cecie's escape. Then she remembered her old grievances.

"You are a fine one to be lecturing me! I am

177

surprised that you even noticed that I was missing. I expected you to be consoling your Marie."

"Marie can manage quite well without my consolation," he said uneasily.

"Even when there is so little time left? I would have thought that you would have made the most of every minute."

" 'Little time left'? She said that?" Peter asked with keen interest.

"Yes, she was most distraught!"

"She must have been to let something like that slip out."

"Perhaps you should hurry to her now and hold her hand while you can still have a few hours together!"

"Shame on you, you are beginning to sound common, Cecie. Did she say why there was no time?"

"No!" she snapped, stamping her foot.

"Cecie! This ill becomes you!"

Despite her anger, she was stung by the justice of his retort. "I suppose that I am very tired," she murmured, leaning against the wall for support again.

"We both are. It is time to go home." He slipped his arm around her shoulders and squeezed them comfortingly, then kissed her full on the lips. "There, now we are at peace."

"Peter! What if someone sees us?"

"It no longer matters!"

"It certainly does! They will become suspicious of us and never let us leave France!"

"We are no longer waiting for their permission. Just this night I have obtained help from a friend. Tomorrow he will arrange for horses to be waiting for us along the road to the coast, and I have got word to Willie that the *Mary Ann* is to be ready to sail on the instant. We will slip away day after tomorrow and be in England before you can blink an eye."

"What of the information you sought?"

"I will just have to leave without it, a pity since something seems to be happening at last. . . ."

"Count Talleyrand!" Cecie simpered in French, punching Peter in the stomach before she swooped into a curtsy.

"Mlle. Pendyne! I have been searching for you the whole of the evening. You must give an old friend the pleasure of your company. This time I really must insist that your brother relinquish all claims."

Peter had executed a hasty bow. "You are kind to pay such attention to my little sister, sir, but we would not place such demands on you."

A pained look crossed the other man's face. "Demands? The only demands are those *I* make for her company, Monsieur Pendyne. It is I who am demanding, not your sister. I insist!" Smiling and bowing, he took Cecie's hand, placed it on his own, and turned back to Peter.

Peter refused to give up. "But I was just going to return my sister to the comfortable home you have so generously provided for us We had plans to rise early tomorrow."

"But tomorrow you can sleep late. The trip to Malmaison is the following day. That will be a delightful outing, I am sure. I only regret that I will be unable to accompany you."

"Malmaison?"

"Of course. You are part of the party going there, are you not?"

"We are?"

"Yes, Peter, we are."

"I hadn't realized. . . ."

"So I see." Talleyrand was looking at him closely.

Cecie, catching sight of Peter's grim expression caused by such bad news, hastened to draw attention to herself. "I am so looking forward to seeing the Empress's estate and gardens. I understand that the grounds of Malmaison are magnificent."

"Yes, Her Majesty has imported rare and wonderful trees and shrubs to plant around her country home. And the rose gardens are magnificent." He was walking slowly back toward the ballroom and Cecie leaned on his arm, chattering away. Peter was forgotten.

"It is such a pity that you won't be there to point them out to me."

"I am desolate that business makes that impossible, Mlle. Cecie. I can think of no greater happiness than leading you through the maze of Malmaison. Some say that it takes hours to find one's way out, it is so cunningly contrived. And it has the most charming little benches scattered

180

throughout it, at just the right places to pause and rest."

"How lovely! I find the French countryside fascinating. I am so looking forward to seeing more of it."

"I hope that I will be your guide on another occasion."

Cecie, entertaining a sudden happy thought of her own, kept the conversation firmly on the topic of France and her districts, especially those to the north that surrounded such ports as Dieppe. She thought she saw the count's eyes widen slightly when she mentioned that city, then he continued to answer her questions with all of his considerable charm, and she could not be sure that she had not imagined it.

Meanwhile, Peter, left behind in the hall, had put his mind furiously to work on this new obstacle to their escape. Malmaison?

Twenty

The following morning, Mme. de Moncy called very early. Cecie felt that one more spy had been added to the ranks of her household, but with a sigh she set about entertaining the lady as best she could in Peter's absence. She kept reminding herself that Mme. de Moncy's ambitions were all selfish.

"Monsieur Pierre is not here?" the lady asked for the third time.

"No, my brother was called to an interview with Count Talleyrand early this morning. I understand that he will be there most of the day."

"But I must speak to him!"

"But I myself was unable to talk with him before he left, Madam." A very early summons, a sudden burst of activity in the gardens on the part of their outdoors staff, the hovering of a suddenly solicitous housekeeper, had made it impossible for them to converse.

Cecie watched as the lady before her twisted her handkerchief and fidgeted about in a fit of anxiety. To fill the silence, she continued the nonsense she had inflicted on the Frenchwoman but the evening before. Mme. de Moncy seemed not to hear.

"It is so important that I see him as soon as possible, Mlle. Pendyne. There is not much time before he returns and someone has sent him word. . . ."

"Who is to return?"

"My husband." In her distressed state of mind she did not realize at first what she had said to the girl.

"And when will he arrive, Mme. de Moncy?" Cecie asked with bright interest.

The older woman saw her mistake too late and glanced at Cecie sharply. There was only a look of fatuous interest for her to see. "It is just that we are preparing a surprise for my dearest husband, Mademoiselle. It is imperative that all this be kept secret," she said glibly.

"Of course! I shan't tell a soul! How marvelous for him. Will he be staying in Paris long?"

Sure that the girl believed her, the Frenchwoman relaxed. "He will stay here only long enough to be given the dispatches for Austria."

"And then he will be off again. What a pity that you can't have a longer visit with him. It must be exciting to be married to such an important man."

Her guest grimaced. "Very exciting."

"And what shall I tell my brother?"

"Just that it is imperative that he come to me. I must see him." A belated sense of caution again assailed her. "Just that, mind you! He will understand."

Cecie, who was suspicious of all she had heard, smiled even more sweetly. "But of course. I will tell him exactly that and no more. You can rely on me."

Peter had returned very late that night, long after the housekeeper had driven Cecie off to bed with her unwanted company. They did not see each other until the arrival of their carriage for the drive to Malmaison.

The coach was a landau and Cecie found herself enjoying the play of the breeze and sunlight on her dress and pelisse, her parasol casting ineffective but interesting shadows over the interior of the open coach. She grimaced up at the coachman and groom who were attending them, able to hear every word she spoke.

"A lovely day for a picnic, is it not, Peter?" she asked in English.

"Lovely."

She thought she caught a look of comprehension on the face of the groom, a young man who though sturdily built did not fit her idea of a servant. His manners were too self assured, his looks too polished, for her to conceive of him as anything but their spy in chief.

"The gardens will be beautiful."

"Quite."

"Do say something beyond a single word every

185

time I put an unexceptional comment to you, Peter!" she said with quick irritation, speaking very fast.

He smiled at her and answered her with a heavy Cornish accent. "If I can't say what I want, I shall say nothing at all, love."

She glanced sharply at the groom and caught a look of resentful bewilderment. "Do you fear that the plans for the picnic will go awry?" she asked calmly in French, placing heavy emphasis on the word picnic in the hope that he would sense her double meaning. She had been cudgeling her brain all morning to determine how they were going to effect their escape in the face of such thorough guardians. And he did not yet know of her small subterfuge over Dieppe.

"I think that if the weather holds, all should go well."

Giving him a quick look, she liked what she saw and relaxed against the upholstered cushions of the landau, sure that he had things well in hand.

Although how he was going to manage it she didn't know. They were deep in enemy territory, closely watched, surrounded by the pomp and authority of the French government. The clothes they wore, the carriage they rode in, the servants about them, the roof over their heads, even the food they ate, were granted them on sufferance, a sufferance that could as easily have been withdrawn without a moment's notice. It was strange that now she should regain her faith in him, after days of racking doubts. They must be able to flee with haste when the moment came, if they were to have any chance of succeeding, and she would follow him without question.

But the day around them cried out for a slow, relaxed outlook on life. They arrived at Malmaison at the appointed hour, one of a caravan of guests. People swarmed around them as soon as they stepped out and she gave up her quest for a private moment with him.

Cecie could not but help enjoy what she saw around her. The gardens and lawns of the grounds were extensive and beautifully planned and kept, and the house itself was charming, nestled among the trees and shrubs. A clever imagination had been at work there.

The spot chosen for the picnic could be easily discerned by the billowing striped canvas awnings that had been erected over the tables where they were to sit and eat later that day, the colors of the stripes lending to the festive air of the scene. Birds sang around them, paths branched out with alluring twists and turns, the sky was blue and the sun's heat mitigated by the gentle breeze that stirred Cecie's hair and parasol. It would all make for a delightful day for the girl, except for one thing: this was France, not England. Then some perverse imp in her mind made her swear to herself that she would remember in detail what she saw that day and duplicate it as best she could, when she could, someplace in England. From this promise she derived immense satisfaction, and began to take a fascinated interest in all that went on around her, much to Peter's disgust.

The maze was quite as complicated as the count had warned her, and she and another happy couple spent a cheerful hour in it before the picnic spread was placed on the tables. The sound of the musicians tuning up to play during the luncheon lured them away from the maze, on the insistence of their hungry male escort who was far more interested in the cold chicken, ham, duck, fruit, pastries and wine.

During the frivolous activities of the day, Cecie had a sharp sense of urgency beneath her calm. Peter had hinted that all would be well, and if so, she would be in England, in Cornwall with her parents, in a few days. How he would do it was a mystery to her. From time to time she pinched herself to be sure that it wasn't just a dream, that she wouldn't awake in her strange tent bed. Only the presence of so many French soldiers resplendent in their uniforms with pistols and muskets and sabers, reminded her of the danger lurking all around her. Everywhere she looked, even while in the middle of the ornamental lake being paddled about by a rather elderly admirer and a young naval lieutenant, she saw evidence of military force. No amount of rationalizing that this was to be expected, that they were there to protect Her Majesty, could soothe her on this count.

Her nerves were drawn taut by the time the servants made an effort to begin cleaning up the debris left by the picnickers. When was Peter going to act? What was she to do?

She was looking around her in an agitated fashion hoping to catch a glimpse of Peter, when the elderly man ambled off and left her with the naval officer.

"You must go to him along the path that leads to the fountain beyond the maze," her companion said unexpectedly in English.

"Heaven save me!" Cecie said without thinking, using the same language. "Who are you?"

"I am an old friend of Peter's from his days in the Quartier Latin. I saw him last night at the ball."

Cecie looked closely at the aristocratic face of the man standing before her and was reassured. His eyes were open and honest and his smile convincing. She was almost sure of his story as a truthful one, but common sense held her back. He began grinning when he sensed the tiny doubt gnawing at her mind.

"Peter said that by his oath at the Holy Well, he would get you out of France this night. You are to meet him on the lane beyond the fountain. He will be waiting there with horses and a change of raiment. Now hurry. We have left it until almost too late, that boring old man wouldn't take himself off."

"The Holy Well? Only Peter and I know of that. Thank heavens it is at last beginning to happen. I was dying all day with suspense."

He bowed and offered her his arm, indicating that he would accompany her. "They will notice it less if we leave together. Everyone will think it is a little privacy we are seeking, a few

189

moments alone together. And what could be more natural, a gentleman in the company of such a beautiful woman?"

Cecie, who had heard more than enough fulsome compliments in the course of her stay in France, had decided that a Frenchman would be spouting sweet nothings in any circumstances, at any time. She also thought that this time she didn't mind in the least. "Won't they be suspicious when I don't return with you?"

"I will tell them that you were leading me such a merry chase that I lost you in the trees. They will never doubt it, for I shall be quite heartbroken, I assure you."

"You are very good to help us in this way," she said impulsively, as they moved past the hedges of the maze.

"Not at all," he answered. "I am enchanted to have finally made your acquaintance, Mlle. Cecilia. I have quite enjoyed my afternoon."

He sounded as if he meant it, and Cecie couldn't help but grin at him. "I have enjoyed myself, too, Lieutenant de Montfort. I will always remember this afternoon, though I live to be a hundred."

His expression was suddenly serious. "Look, there he is, through those bushes."

Peter was waiting for them impatiently on a lane and Cecie was flung into her saddle without being allowed to change into the riding habit he had so thoughtfully provided. "We have little time. They will soon begin to leave, and then your absence will be noted, Cecie."

"Never fear, Pierre," their friend said with a smile. "These things take a very long time to sort out. Someone important will lose a scarf or a shawl and everyone will have to stop what they are doing to hunt for it."

"We can't count on that, André," Peter said grimly.

"Oh, yes, we can." He pulled a piece of gauze from his pocket and dangled it before their eyes. Cecie recognized it before Peter, and began to laugh.

"Oh, you darling man, you have taken her favorite scarf! Shame on you."

"What are you talking about?" Peter said, bewildered.

"It is the Empress's scarf, Peter. Everyone will be hunting for it."

"And I shall win her good graces by being the one to find it, which might be useful if they choose to frown on me for losing Cecilia," André added.

Peter, much tried by the events of the last few days, stared from one laughing face to the other, shaking his head with exasperation. "I don't understand, but no matter, we'd best be off. God bless you, André, for helping us."

"Thank you very much!" Cecie added.

"The pleasure was entirely mine, Mlle. Cecilia. It is I who should be thanking you." And there he stood in the dust, giving her one last flirtatious bow. "Good luck!"

"We must move fast if we are to outstrip our

pursuers, Cecie," Peter said anxiously about an hour later when his cousin began to slow her mount. "We have very little time. We must get to the *Mary Ann* before the French soldiers watching her are reinforced. I told Willie to take care of them as best he could, but he can't take on the entire French army."

"It is all that fat old baron's fault, Peter. We could not get away from him."

"Be that as it may, they will be on our trail soon enough."

"No, they won't."

"Don't be foolish."

"They will be heading north."

"What?"

"I kept asking Talleyrand about Dieppe at the ball. You just see if I am not right. When they notice that we are gone, they will start checking the roads to the north. How clever it was of you to think to leave from the party. I would have hated to miss it altogether."

He grinned ruefully at this last, but did not comment on it. "The position of the estate west of Paris gave me the idea, love. It meant we would be one step on our journey. How clever of you to discuss Dieppe with Talleyrand."

"Well, I did promise to help, didn't I?"

"That is true."

"Now, I must stop and change my clothes, I think those bushes over there will do nicely. I don't want to ruin this lovely party dress, you know. It will just take a minute. By the way,

192

General de Moncy was carrying dispatches to Austria."

"What?"

"*She* told me so yesterday. Does knowing that help?"

"It certainly does!" Swallowing hard on his laughter, he accepted the reins of her mount and waited for a minute, or perhaps two, for her to return to him more suitably attired for the grueling ride ahead of them.

Twenty-one

They reached the *Mary Ann* when the tide was still flooding in, a matter that caused Peter to break into strong oaths. Cecie failed to remind him that it was impolite to do so in the presence of a young lady, for they had ridden through the night and she was beyond caring. Willie hustled her down into the cabin, made her as comfortable as he could, then returned to the deck where the yacht's captain, still cursing, was making everything ready for setting sail, even if it meant fighting against the tide. The dawn was breaking in the east, but the sea to the west was still dark and threatening; if they could just clear the inlet they had a chance of escaping into the Channel before the French patrols spotted them in the increasing light.

When the ship lurched into the channel of the creek, Cecie found herself wide awake and crept onto the deck. In the fury of activity involved in getting the ship clear, no one noticed her, and she found a vantage point from which she could watch without impeding the work. A magnificent sunrise was spreading over the horizon, and a soft land breeze wafted the fragrance of green grass and soil while it filled the sails of the *Mary Ann*.

Hope rose in her heart as she realized that the *Mary Ann* was beginning to make way down the creek. The tide had turned in time after all, and the breeze helped the ship's progress. There was every chance of escaping the inlet for the Baie de la Seine, and finding their way into the Channel and home, if only nothing would interfere. They moved slowly, painfully down the creek.

As they cleared the mouth of the inlet, ominous sails appeared on the horizon. No matter what flag they carried, they belonged to the enemy. A sailor shouted to Peter, who still demanded to know the flag. Cecie supposed that there might be some comfort in knowing who their destroyers were. Then when the word came that she was French, Peter gave a stream of orders and the *Mary Ann* turned to the west, away from the oncoming ships.

Cecie gathered her courage and approached him near the wheel. "What difference does it make who they are, Peter? They will fire on us in any case, whether French or English."

"The French certainly will, love. No doubt orders were sent to all the ports long since to watch for us, and I would guess that Havre de Grâce has been on a special alert."

"Is that where they are from, Havre de Grâce?"

"Yes. Now, you must get back down into the cabin. You will be safer there than anyplace here on deck. If they score any hits, the splinters will fly. That is the worst danger in a sea battle."

"I would rather watch and know what is happening, Peter. It would be better to die in the open."

"Die?" He was laughing at her. "No one is going to die if I can help it. We'll pull through this one, love."

"I would still rather smell the sea air than stay in that stuffy cabin," she protested.

"Well, stay a while longer, Cecie. But you must promise me that if their shots come near us, you will retire below, if for no other reason than our need on deck for all the freedom of action we can achieve. Your presence might hamper us, if only by distracting the men with a concern for your safety."

Cecie looked as if she were going to argue this point, but then a glance around showed her that the men were staring at her. Peter was right. When the action came, if it came, she would go below.

"Do we have a chance of outrunning them, Peter?"

"Not much of one without a little luck, Cecie. They carry more sail and are designed for speed. But we can stay close to the shore and remain out of their reach, and there are creeks and rivers to slip into and hide."

"But won't that bring us up to Cherbourg? We are caught between them."

"I have planned this better than that, love."

For the next hour it seemed that Peter's predictions would hold true. The French ships did fire on them once, only to gauge the range, according to Willie, who had been appointed her protector for the time being. The range was obviously well beyond their guns, and the balls fell into the water many hundreds of yards off their stern. But fear still clutched Cecie, and she knew that the larger ships were lumbering closer and closer, having the stronger winds of the open bay to give them speed. She appreciated that the *Mary Ann* was far more maneuverable in close quarters than the French vessels bearing down on them, but in the open sea she stood no chance. And it would be necessary to cross the open sea to reach England.

Another shout drew her attention to the starboard quarter. There, out in the bay, two more sails had appeared from the direction of Cherbourg. Peter examined them with his spyglass, then demanded from the sailor in the topmost shroud if they carried the English flag. The wind blew the answer away, but Cecie knew that they now had two enemies to contend with. They were caught between grinding rocks, and their only hope was that the British and French captains would ignore the *Mary Ann* and go after one another.

A slight shift in the deck of the craft warned her that they were changing tack, and Peter seemed to be very sure of the orders he gave. She took heart, thinking that he had some clever strategy planned, a strategy that would carry them away from their double danger. Then with a sinking sensation that had nothing to do with the tossing of the sea, she saw that they were heading straight for the English ships.

"Peter, no, no, you mustn't let them catch you!"

"But that is exactly what I must do, love. Don't worry, I know what I am about."

"But Peter, they will throw you into prison as soon as they lay hands on you. They will clap you into chains and carry you off. Peter, I couldn't bear it if anything happened to you."

He stopped his pacing and faced her, startled to see tears in her eyes. "Cecie, Cecie, don't cry! All will be well. You must have greater faith in me."

"You are doing this for my sake. If the English ships catch us, they will see to it that I get home, no matter what happens to you."

"Yes, they would get you back to your parents. But you needn't worry. I intend to do that little chore myself. I think your father will want to have a long talk with me."

She ignored the half rueful, half teasing tone in his voice and cried all the more. "I would rather live in France than have you captured! Please, please, turn back, there must be another way."

His arms were around her and she was sobbing on his shoulder, when the sound of more gunfire startled them into an awareness of their surroundings. Now the English ships had rolled out their guns, and fired to estimate the range. Only they were much closer than the French had been, and the *Mary Ann* was directly in the path of their cannonballs. "They are going to shoot us!" she gasped.

"Wait and see. Willie, did you get that signal up as I told you to?"

"Aye, sir. She be up that high, like you said."

"Two points to starboard, helmsman," he ordered.

"That will take us directly across their path."

"And it will lead the French into better range."

"We shall be pulverized!"

"I don't think so. The *Melpomene* has a greater range than either of the French tubs. Her guns will hit them far sooner that they will reach her."

"But the French will soon be upon us! They are closing in fast on the tail of the *Mary Ann.*"

"That is called the stern, love." Before he could continue his nautical instructions, more fire was heard from the *Melpomene*. The smaller sloop that was dancing attendance on her was still silent. To Cecie's surprise and relief, the shot went well over their heads and missed the small yacht's sails.

"They may hit us by mistake."

"No, we will soon be out of her way. Besides, the *Mary Ann* is so much smaller than the *Melpomene,* they would have to aim down to hit us."

200

"The sloop will have no such problem," Cecie protested.

"No, not if she wants to aim at us."

"If? Is she not the very ship that chased us into the French creek in the first place? It is she who fired on the *Mary Ann* and damaged her. If it weren't for that sloop, we would not have been stranded in France!"

Peter smiled at her indignation. "Then we would have missed our adventure, Cecie."

"And they would never have known that you smuggled!" She was near to tears again, but Peter turned back to the helm and was rapping out more orders. "Don't you care?"

"Cecie, love, there are many things of which you are ignorant. I will soon be able to explain it all to you, but dash it, will you please have a little more faith in me? I am not a total fool!"

Stung by the exasperation in his voice, she turned on her heel and stalked down into the cabin, there to nurse her grievances. To her surprise, no one attempted to board the *Mary Ann*; she could only guess that the English captains were so sure of their firepower that they were willing to rely on that threat to assure compliance. The yacht shifted again as she made another change in tack, and Cecie thought they were heading more northeast now, but she was not sure that she cared. Peter had said he had the matter well in hand, she was only in the way. Very well, she would leave him to his own destruction. So be it.

*   *   *

In her anger, Cecie missed several interesting events. The sloop, far from presenting a warlike appearance once the *Mary Ann* was safe behind the huge *Melpomene,* was positively friendly. In fact, shouts of welcome were exchanged when they drew near enough, and much chaffing could be heard between the two young men in command of the vessels.

And there, sitting to one side of the cabin, was a large trunk, carefully tied, with a slip of paper bearing her own name attached. If she had thought to look more carefully, if she had noticed it at all, she would have seen that it was of French make and design. And if she had attempted to lift it, she would have found it heavy and full.

Twenty-two

Their escort directed them to Dover, as Cecie had feared it would, and she was set on dry land late that afternoon. Peter soon stood beside her, apparently in the best of spirits; he must have been ignoring her tearful countenance and determined silence to have maintained such a happy disposition. They were duly met by an army officer of the rank of colonel, a fact that impressed itself on Cecie sensibly, for surely they would have sent some lesser personage for an ordinary criminal? She feared that this boded ill for Peter, and when they were bundled into a chaise and four with very little comment from their guardian, she was sure of it. They were soon lumbering onto the London–Dover road, making good time in their conveyance and stopping frequently for fresh horses. A slower cart followed them at its own pace, piled high with this and that from the *Mary Ann*.

As they drove into the lowering darkness, her

cousin somehow found the savoir-faire necessary to make idle comments on the passing countryside, to which the colonel responded in glum monosyllables. Cecie wasn't sure if she should laugh or weep at Peter's cheery, commonplace civilities. Her inclination was toward the latter.

She went over the list of charges against him. Smuggling: undoubtedly. The existence of the *Mary Ann,* too well built and crewed for mere pleasure, was one proof, the presence of the vessel, with captain and crew, in French waters, was another, and the loaded cart, which she had seen just as they pulled out of the dock area at Dover, convinced her that irrefutable proof was at hand.

Spying: perhaps. If she were careful in what she said, no one need know of the friendly interest taken by Talleyrand and the Emperor himself. Their detention need have taken them no farther afield than the Courseulles district, for all they would hear from her. And the fact that they had been detained was a point in their favor. She would make much of Captain Duval; the mansion and parties had best be forgotten.

Kidnapping: never, not as long as she had breath in her. Her presence on the *Mary Ann* was a misfortune she now freely laid at her own door. She had been foolhardy to invade Peter's boat and had paid the consequences. The absurdity of her act of falling asleep made her blush. Kidnapping would not be proved on her evidence.

As she was dozing off a new and disturbing

thought entered her mind. What would people call it? If not kidnapping, what? She thought of other cases when a young couple had disappeared for more than a day. What had it been called then? When it involved Miss Lucille Framby and that regrettable Lieutenant Delroy, the word elopement had been bandied about.

Elopement? It was most improper. Papa would never approve, Mama would be shocked. She felt herself blushing as she toyed with the word. Elopement? But didn't that mean that she was ruined? Only marriage would redeem her. And on this lowering thought, she drifted off into exhausted slumber.

The bed they had put her in was very soft, the coverlet made of silk, the sheets sweet and dry. She was in the home of gentlefolk, she was sure, not some common inn. She stirred unhappily, trying to recapture the vagrant thought that had been teasing her when she fell asleep, but it eluded her. Then she was fully awake.

It *was* a very handsome bedchamber. The sunlight poured in through a window on the other side of the room, a window frilled with ruched curtains. A tree branch tapped the panes of glass. She thought it was this sound that had awakened her, not the bright suffusion of light.

She groped for the bellpull and found it. It was answered with gratifying promptness by a respectable-looking woman of middle years, who bobbed a curtsy and then turned to fetch a ladened tray from some unseen resting place in the hall. Cecie found herself being fussed over, her pillows plumped up, the coverlet straightened, the tray put in place before her. She lacked the courage to ask the maid where she was, and in truth the woman turned to leave before the girl had much opportunity to frame her questions. But at the door, the woman curtsied again and warned her that Lady Morley would soon be up to visit her. At least one question was answered.

She applied herself to the breakfast, finding that she had a hearty appetite and hoping that Peter had fared half as well. She had already demolished the ham when the door was opened.

The lady who entered the room was a stranger to her, but for all this Cecie was greeted in the friendliest fashion possible.

"Dear Lady Cecilia, I am so glad that you are awake. I hope that you have suffered no ill effects from your adventure? I am Lady Morley, as perhaps Griselda has told you, and I am glad to offer you my hospitality here in London until your parents arrive. What a marvelous hairstyle! Is that all the crack in Paris?"

Cecie put one hesitant hand to her head. She had no idea what her hair looked like at that moment, but since she had seen the hairdresser and had her curls shorn under the tutelage of Count Talleyrand in Paris, she supposed that it was all the crack. "I had it done while in. . . ." She had almost been caught in a dangerous confession. Drat her unwary tongue!

"In Paris, of course," Lady Morley finished for
206

her on a crowing note. "Mr. Pendyne has told us all about that!"

"Oh, dear!"

Her hostess was instantly all solicitude. "You needn't worry, Lady Cecilia. We have taken every step we could to see that no one hears of your sojourn there with your cousin. He has explained that you passed as brother and sister and his word as a gentleman is enough to convince us all that that describes the nature of your relationship there exactly. Your good name will suffer no harm."

Cecie had had other worries. "Good name?" She had forgotten.

"You are very young, aren't you?" Cecie's innocence seemed to reassure the lady far more than Peter's word had done, despite her protests to the contrary. "Evil tongues would make much of it, if they knew. But we shall say that you have been visiting with me here in Park Lane, but were laid up with a fever. We will set it about that you came up to see the dressmakers under my guidance, then caught some slight ill. That will account for no one seeing you, although there is no one about to see you in any case. It is fortunate that there are so few people in Town just now."

Cecie's head was begining to whirl under the impact of this reasoning and she tendered one question. "But why should I be visiting you?"

"I am your mother's second cousin, of course. Didn't you know? I suppose not, you have lived

207

such a retired life down there in Cornwall. It is all quite unexceptional."

Unexceptional if you discounted the fact that Cecie hadn't the least idea of what Lady Morley was talking about. Were they discussing the same situation? What had happened to Peter? "Most fortunate."

"Yes, isn't it?"

"But how did you come to be so invloved in all this?"

"Morley, of course. Hasn't Peter told you? He is Peter's godfather, you know."

"No, I didn't know." Cecie mulled this over in silence, appreciating the advantages that such a godfather would bring to Peter, given his present situation.

"It was my youngest son Rupert who captained the sloop, you see."

"The sloop? The one that damaged the *Mary Ann*?"

"Yes. Wasn't it clever of them?" Before Cecie could answer this amazing comment, the maid entered the room and murmured a word in her mistress's ear.

"Oh, dear, there is someone downstairs demanding to see you. He says that he is a connection of yours and knows all. It would seem that he has come to rescue you!"

"I have already been rescued quite sufficiently, I think."

"I do so agree. But I will just see to him. Won't you join us when you have finished your meal and made your toilette?"

Cecie, driven by curiosity, wolfed down her food and began tearing at the only dress she could find in the wardrobe, the afternoon costume she had worn to Malmaison. She looked at the fine French workmanship and decided that it would have to do, although it positively screamed its foreign origin. No matter.

When she entered the library somewhat more quickly than was her wont, she beheld an awful sight indeed. There, resplendent in his full regimentals and the authority they gave him, his face looking angry and suspicious, was Major Hugh Armstrong.

"Cecie, there you are. Come in and straighten out this confusion. I am fully aware of what happened and I will settle for nothing less than the truth."

She couldn't escape. On tiptoe, she advanced to the major. "Major Armstrong." She gave him two fingers, the barest that courtesy allowed, and made a slight bow.

"We have all been grievously concerned for your safety, although your parents tried to put a brave face on it. No one is fooled by the story they put about. You had best tell me all so that I can help you."

Lady Morley had appeared behind the major and was giving her guest a grimace of encouragement and comfort. "What story, Major Armstrong?"

"The story that in the middle of the night Cecie saw fit to go visit her Aunt Pendyne. Absurd."

Lady Morley laughed. "Yes, it is absurd. She obviously has come to visit me. I wonder if you did not get the story confused, major?"

Cecie, taking heart and feeling not a little angry, added her mite. "I only stopped at Aunt Pendyne's for a night on the road, Major Armstrong."

"Then that must be the source of the confusion," Lady Morley agreed.

Armstrong was beginning to bluster as he faced two smiling women who were determined not to tell him what he already knew for fact. "You went off with Peter Pendyne on some madcap adventure and have only returned to England this past night."

"I say you are wrong, sir," Lady Morley said in a level tone.

"On the contrary. I know that I am right. I have had men watching the ports and they saw her disembark yesterday afternoon. Disembark from the *Mary Ann,* in the company of her cousin, an unprincipled scoundrel who had taken advantage of her innocence and carried her off. We must act quickly to salvage what we can of her reputation."

"You needn't be so anxious to offer your help, Hugh," Cecie began to say with some heat.

"For her reputation is quite intact. She spent the past several days here under my roof," Lady Morley finished for her.

"When did she arrive?" Armstrong shot out at her.

"I will not have my word questioned in my

own home, major. My footman will show you the way out." She reached for a bellpull and tugged.

"I am not leaving without Cecie."

"Now, that *would* be highly improper, sir. You overreach yourself."

"On the contrary. Her only hope is to be married quickly to a man of good repute, such as myself. I have the special license here in my pocket and will take the necessary actions immediately to see that we are wed."

"I would sooner marry a horny toad than you, Hugh Armstrong! You are quite insufferable, you, you. . . ." Here it was fortunate that a footman did arrive, a very husky one, and this cut short Cecie's tirade before it descended into unlady-like language. To his chagrin, Major Armstrong discovered that he had been outflanked.

"I will not give this up, Lady Morley. I intend to save this young woman despite herself."

"Your comments are unwarranted, unbecoming, and impertinent, sir. Leave!"

With the burly footman at his elbow, he was forced to turn toward the door. Then the sound of many voices in the hallway stopped him. The door opened, revealing Lord and Lady Penrith, with Peter in their shadow. In a trice, Cecie was crying in her mother's arms.

Twenty-three

The arrival of Peter and her parents was almost an anticlimax for poor Cecie. Hugh's words had left their mark and she had wrung the last iota of emotion from herself in a frenzy of self abnegation and anxiety. She even thought of making the ultimate sacrifice and marrying a man whom she abhorred. Or would it be simpler to run away? If this would save some part of the situation, protect Peter from the retribution his actions demanded, save her parents from scandal, she would do it. It was with this frame of mind that she faced the three people she most cared for.

"Cecie, darling, you are all right!" Lady Penrith said as her daughter's sobbing subsided.

"Peter took good care of me."

Armstrong snorted. "That is far from being the case, my lady. Cecie's situation is quite untenable. I have prepared for the only course of action that will salvage something from this debacle; the special license is right here in my pocket."

"It was all my fault, Papa, for sneaking on board the boat. You mustn't blame Peter."

"I would imagine that no such course of action would have occurred to you if you had not somehow become aware of his smuggling activities, or whatever they were," Hugh argued.

"I should have faced him squarely in a more sensible manner, or told Papa about it," she answered with spirit.

Lord Penrith surprised the two combatants. "Do stop this nonsense. It has turned out well enough and we can soon return home. Cecie is safe. That is what counts."

"Sir!" Armstrong's voice told of the depths of his shock.

"Do take yourself off, Hugh. Your presence here is not needed," Penrith answered. "And stop these nonsensical charges. No one will believe them, in any case." He took the officer by the arm and showed him the door. The atmosphere lightened perceptibly with Armstrong's departure.

Lord Penrith mopped his brow and said to no one, "Although it seems monstrous that a gentleman must stoop to spying."

Peter smiled and answered. "Someone had to do it, sir, and I seemed a likely choice. I speak French and know my way about that country. My old friend Rupert Morley suggested it to me, and I leapt at the chance. It was an opportunity to really do something to avert the danger that

England was facing. It had been damned flat sitting around while others defended her."

"Defended her? You mean you were working for England?" Cecie asked.

"Of course."

"You aren't in trouble?"

"No, I have never been, at least not with the English government. They have known and approved of all my actions. Lord Morley has even been so kind as to take steps to cover your absence when it was discovered. I had warned him earlier that you suspected my activities and he managed to guess what had happened, especially after he heard what Molly had to say. We were all surprised that you stumbled on the smuggling. I had not foreseen that."

"Whyever not foresee it? Even Hugh Armstrong guessed that something was afoot." She was beginning to nurse a real sense of grievance against him. Against the Morleys. Against the government. How dare they not tell her?

"He was supposed to. We could rely on his heavy handed snooping to convince the French that I was in earnest and facing some danger at home. It was important for my credentials."

"And the government knew of all this?"

"Yes."

She had risen to her feet, back to the fire burning in the grate. There was a challenge in her stance, for all her ladylike appearance. "Did they know about Mme. de Moncy, too?"

"Mme. de Moncy?" her father asked with confusion.

"Mme. de Moncy. Peter spent the whole of his time in Paris making a fool of himself with that woman. It was shocking! I do not know how he can show his face to us!"

The Penriths turned to stare at Peter, expressions of well-bred interest, never curiosity, on their faces.

"She was an important source of information," he protested.

"Do you expect anyone to believe that?" Cecie stormed. The room was silent. Now her parents were regarding her with that same well-bred interest. Cecie could bear it no longer and turned to the door in tears. "He is horrible, horrible. I shall marry Hugh Armstrong, just you wait and see," were the last words she flung over her shoulder. Her father moved as if to follow her, but Lady Penrith restrained him with a smile.

"I quite appreciate that Lord Morley has vouched for you, Peter, and I have even accepted your assurances as to the, ah, nature of your relationship with Cecie while in Paris, with the understanding that the two of you are to wed in any case, but who is Mme. de Moncy?" the irate father asked.

"She was the wife of an important staff officer serving along the coast. I had met her in the days I was a student in Paris, when she was but newly wed. It had occured to me that her husband's movements would be some indication of the Emperor's plans as regarded the invasion, so I, uh, cultivated her, I suppose you might say."

"Cecie does not seem to understand that," the older man thundered.

"Yes, sir. I mean, no, sir."

"You can't very well marry her if she chooses that fool Armstrong, boy. You have mismanaged this badly!"

"Yes, sir."

"Then you must go to her and explain," Lady Penrith said, a hint of amusement in her voice. Lady Morley nodded her agreement.

"She won't listen," her husband grumbled.

"I think she will. Now go to her."

Peter found his cousin sobbing her heart out in a small, little-used parlor. She was stung by the turn of events; her whole heart and soul had been convinced of something, learned to accept it after much pain and travail, only to be told that it was not so. She had been duped, made a fool of, by someone she trusted. Well, she would never make that mistake again.

Peter caught something of her mood and looked at her anxiously. "Are you so very angry at me, Cecie? I do not know how else I could have managed the thing."

"You might have told me the truth!" Her rigid dignity warned him that the situation was very serious indeed.

"But your conviction that I was guilty made the plan a success! Without you, I fear that I would have failed."

A frown of suspicion crossed her face. "I wish

someone would tell me what this is all about. What plan?"

He smiled, relieved to see the old Cecie reappearing. "The plan to convince Napoleon that he really ought to invade Austria."

The frown deepened.

"My part was to feed him false information on the readiness of our coastal defenses. The French believed that my so-called smuggling activities gave them some power over me, and they believed most of what I told them."

Her interest was captured and she began to unravel the threads of the tale. "So you were not telling them the truth?"

"Far from it."

"And you said what the gentlemen of the government wanted you to say?"

"Exactly. They knew everything that I did. In fact, I never made a move without their express orders." Which was perhaps not precisely the truth, Peter thought to himself, but the situation demanded extraordinary conduct.

"And they told Lady Morley's son to shoot his guns at the *Mary Ann*?"

"Yes, they did. I needed an excuse to linger on French soil and it seemed easy enough to arrange for it in that manner. Rupert's guns did little damage to her, but it strengthened the story I was telling the French. If they had suspected otherwise. . . ,"

"Oh, dear! They might have killed you!"

"I wasn't too worried about that. I knew that friends would help me to escape." He had lured her over to a small sofa in a bay window and slipped his arm around her waist, without her seeming to notice.

"I might have made them suspect you! I might have been the cause of the plan failing and of you being captured and executed. With me there hampering you, your escape was that much more difficult." He began to dab at her eyes with his handkerchief, staying the flow of tears.

"But without you I would not have convinced the French gentlemen, love. The Emperor was most impressed with your belief that I was a traitor. And it was you who discovered that the French army was on the move into Austria."

"A poor enough thing. That de Moncy creature would have told you if you'd been there."

"I think not, love. She was very careful about what she told me, but with you she was less guarded. She would never have made such an error in my presence."

"I feel so dreadful. You must have hated me for appearing in the cabin as I did!"

"Never that, love."

He caught her looking at him from under her long lashes. "Why do you keep calling me love?"

"Because you are. You really oughtn't to marry Hugh Armstrong, you know. As a matter of fact, I positively forbid it! I will stand up in church and protest if you are so foolish as to walk with him to the altar."

"Really? Ought you to do that sort of thing?"

"Yes. I want you to marry me. And besides, you don't *want* to marry him. I would strongly advise against it even if my own interest weren't so deeply involved. You will have to settle for me."

"I must?"

"You must. Unless you are taken with his regimentals?" He pulled away from her to watch her more carefully, and suddenly she was laughing.

"Yes, I must marry an officer. After all, with England in a life or death struggle with France, I want to do the patriotic thing."

"I will have to be reinstated in my regiment, instantly! Will that do?"

"Is your uniform as grand as his?"

"Every bit."

"Then I shall do it."

He slipped his arms even more tightly around her waist and was enjoying a satisfactory kiss, when she suddenly struggled to free herself. "What's wrong? Don't you like the way I kiss?" he asked.

"I like it very well indeed. But a young lady doesn't kiss a young man unless she is engaged to him. Properly engaged. Are we?"

"We are." He tried to resume his embrace but she pushed him away again.

"Shouldn't Papa be asked?"

"I have already done so."

"Good."

A minute later she was pulling away again. "Now what is bothering you? Tell me what it is and I shall fix it."

"It is only that I began to think of those dresses

I left back in Paris. I would have looked so glamorous in them! Then you could have been really proud of me when we are in London."

"You mean the French dresses?"

"Of course! They were all to be completed and delivered by LeRoy's the morning we went to Malmaison. What a pity they'll be wasted."

He looked at her with surprise. "Are you sure that is the case? I was told that a very large trunk had been delivered to you on the *Mary Ann*. Didn't you look in it?"

"Trunk?"

"Yes, trunk. You did see one about, didn't you? I could have sworn that it was put on the cart coming to London."

"I saw it in my bedchamber! I will go up and open it." Before he could protest, she had run from the room and could be heard going up the stairs. In a moment she returned, a happy glow on her face.

"They are there! All my lovely French gowns! I shall be a grand success in them! And just look, I found this note from the Empress among them." She opened it up and began to read the contents in silence.

"Damn it, Cecie, aren't you going to share it with me?"

"Gentlemen should not use such language in the presence of a lady," she reprimanded.

"When the lady in question is to be his wife, and when she is being most ungenerous and selfish, which is not the way a bride-to-be should behave, then he has every right to do so. Now, let me see that! I am as curious about it as you are! I wondered about that trunk but I had quite forgotten about it in all the bustle."

He seized the letter and began reading it, only to be interrupted when Cecie wiggled into a position in his arms that enabled her to see the writing too.

Chérie—

I have just sent your things along to Courseulles. I know that you will be leaving France soon and I did not want your lovely gowns left behind! It would have been such a waste. So I told LeRoy that he must get them done instantly, which of course he did. I understand that they are all quite charming.

I hope that these dresses will serve you as a trousseau. A young lady as lovely as you should be married soon. It is a pity that your so handsome brother is just that, your brother. You would have made a magnificent couple!

Josephine

P.S. Talleyrand has been telling me some nonsense about you escaping by way of Dieppe. How foolish men are. Why go there when you want to board your boat in Courseulles?

"I do not believe it! I thought I was so clever telling Talleyrand that we were going to Dieppe,

222

or at least hinting at it. It fooled him, but not the Empress."

"She does seem to have a subtle understanding of what goes on around her," Peter agreed with a grin, rereading the paragraph about the trousseau.

"Well, I am so pleased that she did what she did. I will be the best dressed lady in London! Everyone will be green with envy." Her satisfaction was enormous.

"You will have to thank her one day, Cecie."

"Yes, whenever this dreadful war is at an end. It seems to be lasting forever!"

Peter was not the least bit interested in a discussion of politics and moved to interrupt her. When her parents ventured into the parlor, they found the young couple in happy embrace, wars and dresses forgotten. Lord Penrith didn't understand it all, but his wife led him off to another room, promising to explain it, before he could interrupt.

If you have your heart set on Romance, read
Coventry Romances

THE TULIP TREE—Mary Ann Gibbs	50000–4	$1.75
THE HEARTBREAK TRIANGLE —Nora Hampton	50001–2	$1.75
HELENE—Leonora Blythe	50004–7	$1.75
MEGAN—Norma Lee Clark	50005–5	$1.75
DILEMMA IN DUET—Margaret SeBastian	50003–9	$1.75
THE ROMANTIC WIDOW —Mollie Chappell	50013–6	$1.75

*Let Coventry give you
a little old-fashioned romance.*

8000-3